# DEVIL
## IN A
# BLUE
# DRESS

## WALTER MOSLEY

W·W·NORTON & COMPANY
New York · London

Printed in the United States of America.

*The text of this book is composed in 10/13 Baskerville
with the display set in Varsity.
Composition and manufacturing
by the Haddon Craftsmen, Inc.
Book design by Guenet Abraham.*

First Edition.

Library of Congress Cataloging in Publication Data

Mosley, Walter.
Devil in a blue dress / Walter Mosley.
p. cm.
I. Title.
PS3563.088456D48   1990
813'.54—dc20   89-25503

ISBN 0-393-02854-2

W.W. Norton & Company, Inc.
500 Fifth Avenue, New York, N.Y. 10110
W.W. Norton & Company, Ltd.
37 Great Russell Street, London WC1B 3NU

1 2 3 4 5 6 7 8 9 0

FOR JOY KELLMAN, FREDERIC TUTEN,
AND LEROY MOSLEY

I was surprised to see a white man walk into Joppy's bar. It's not just that he was white but he wore an off-white linen suit and shirt with a Panama straw hat and bone shoes over flashing white silk socks. His skin was smooth and pale with just a few freckles. One lick of strawberry-blond hair escaped the band of his hat. He stopped in the doorway, filling it with his large frame, and surveyed the room with pale eyes; not a color I'd ever seen in a man's eyes. When he looked at me I felt a thrill of fear, but that went away quickly because I was used to white people by 1948.

I had spent five years with white men, and women, from Africa to Italy, through Paris, and into the Fatherland itself. I ate with them and slept with them, and I killed enough blue-eyed young men to know that they were just as afraid to die as I was.

The white man smiled at me, then he walked to the bar where

Joppy was running a filthy rag over the marble top. They shook hands and exchanged greetings like old friends.

The second thing that surprised me was that he made Joppy nervous. Joppy was a tough ex-heavyweight who was comfortable brawling in the ring or in the street, but he ducked his head and smiled at that white man just like a salesman whose luck had gone bad.

I put a dollar down on the bar and made to leave, but before I was off the stool Joppy turned my way and waved me toward them.

"Com'on over here, Easy. This here's somebody I want ya t'meet."

I could feel those pale eyes on me.

"This here's a ole friend'a mines, Easy. Mr. Albright."

"You can call me DeWitt, Easy," the white man said. His grip was strong but slithery, like a snake coiling around my hand.

"Hello," I said.

"Yeah, Easy," Joppy went on, bowing and grinning. "Mr. Albright and me go way back. You know he prob'ly my oldest friend from L.A. Yeah, we go ways back."

"That's right," Albright smiled. "It must've been 1935 when I met Jop. What is it now? Must be thirteen years. That was back before the war, before every farmer, and his brother's wife, wanted to come to L.A."

Joppy guffawed at the joke; I smiled politely. I was wondering what kind of business Joppy had with that man and, along with that, I wondered what kind of business that man could have with me.

"Where you from, Easy?" Mr. Albright asked.

"Houston."

"Houston, now that's a nice town. I go down there sometimes, on business." He smiled for a moment. He had all the time in the world. "What kind of work you do up here?"

Up close his eyes were the color of robins' eggs; matte and dull.

"He worked at Champion Aircraft up to two days ago," Joppy said when I didn't answer. "They laid him off."

Mr. Albright twisted his pink lips, showing his distaste. "That's too bad. You know these big companies don't give a damn about you. The budget doesn't balance just right and they let ten family men go. You have a family, Easy?" He had a light drawl like a well-to-do southern gentleman.

"No, just me, that's all," I said.

"But they don't know that. For all they know you could have ten kids and one on the way but they let you go just the same."

"That's right!" Joppy shouted. His voice sounded like a regiment of men marching through a gravel pit. "Them people own them big companies don't never even come in to work, they just get on the telephone to find out how they money is. And you know they better get a good answer or some heads gonna roll."

Mr. Albright laughed and slapped Joppy on the arm. "Why don't you get us some drinks, Joppy? I'll have scotch. What's your pleasure, Easy?"

"Usual?" Joppy asked me.

"Sure."

When Joppy moved away from us Mr. Albright turned to look around the room. He did that every few minutes, turning slightly, checking to see if anything had changed. There wasn't much to see though. Joppy's was a small bar on the second floor of a butchers' warehouse. His only usual customers were the Negro butchers and it was early enough in the afternoon that they were still hard at work.

The odor of rotted meat filled every corner of the building; there were few people, other than butchers, who could stomach sitting in Joppy's bar.

Joppy brought Mr. Albright's scotch and a bourbon on the rocks for me. He put them both down and said, "Mr. Albright lookin' for a man to do a lil job, Easy. I told him you outta work an' got a mortgage t'pay too."

"That's hard." Mr. Albright shook his head again. "Men in big business don't even notice or care when a working man wants to try to make something out of himself."

"And you know Easy always tryin' t'be better. He just got his high school papers from night school and he been threatenin' on some college." Joppy wiped the marble bar as he spoke. "And he's a war hero, Mr. Albright. Easy went in with Patton. Volunteered! You know he seen him some blood."

"That a fact?" Albright said. He wasn't impressed. "Why don't we go have a chair, Easy? Over there by the window."

Joppy's windows were so dingy that you couldn't see out onto 103rd Street. But if you sat at a small cherry table next to them, at least you had the benefit of the dull glow of daylight.

"You got a mortgage to meet, eh, Easy? The only thing that's worse than a big company is the bank. They want their money on the first and if you miss the payment, they will have the marshal knocking down your door on the second."

"What's my business got to do with you, Mr. Albright? I don't wanna be rude, but I just met you five minutes ago and now you want to know all my business."

"Well, I thought that Joppy said you needed to get work or you were going to lose your house."

"What's that got to do with you?"

"I just might need a bright pair of eyes and ears to do a little job for me, Easy."

"And what kind of work is it that you do?" I asked. I should have gotten up and walked out of there, but he was right about my mortgage. He was right about the banks too.

"I used to be a lawyer when I lived in Georgia. But now I'm just another fella who does favors for friends, and for friends of friends."

"What kind of favors?"

"I don't know, Easy." He shrugged his great white shoulders. "Whatever somebody might need. Let's say that you need to get a message to someone but it's not, um, convenient for you to do it in person; well, then you call me and I take the job. You see I always do the job I'm asked to do, everybody knows that, so I always have lots of work. And sometimes I need a little helper to get the job done. That's where you come in."

"And how's that?" I asked. While he talked it dawned on me that Albright was a lot like a friend I had back in Texas—Raymond Alexander was his name but we called him Mouse. Just thinking about Mouse set my teeth on edge.

"I need to find somebody and I might need a little help looking."

"And who is it you want to—"

"Easy," he interrupted. "I can see that you're a smart man with a lot of very good questions. And I'd like to talk more about it, but not here." From his shirt pocket he produced a white card and a white enameled fountain pen. He scrawled on the card and then handed it to me.

"Talk to Joppy about me and then, if you want to try it out, come to my office any time after seven tonight."

He downed the shot, smiled at me again, and stood up, straightening his cuffs. He tilted the Panama hat on his head and saluted Joppy, who grinned and waved from behind the bar. Then Mr. DeWitt Albright strolled out of Joppy's place like a regular customer going home after his afternoon snort.

The card had his name printed on it in flourished letters. Below that was the address he'd scribbled. It was a downtown address; a long drive from Watts.

I noted that Mr. DeWitt Albright didn't pay for the drinks he ordered. Joppy didn't seem in a hurry to ask for his money though.

**2**

"**W**here'd you meet this dude?"
I asked Joppy.

"I met him when I was still in the ring. Like he said, before the war."

Joppy was still at the bar, leaning over his big stomach and buffing the marble. His uncle, a bar owner himself, had died in Houston ten years earlier, just when Joppy decided to give up the ring. Joppy went all the way back home to get that marble bar. The butchers had already agreed to let him open his business upstairs and all he could think of was getting that marble top. Joppy was a superstitious man. He thought that the only way he could be successful was with a piece of his uncle, already a proven success, on the job with him. Every extra moment Joppy had was spent cleaning and buffing his bar top. He didn't allow roughhousing near the bar and if you ever dropped a pitcher or something heavy he'd be there in a second, looking for chips.

Joppy was a heavy-framed man, almost fifty years old. His hands were like black catcher's mitts and I never saw him in shirt-sleeves that didn't strain at the seams from bulging muscle. His face was scarred from all the punishment he had taken in the ring; the flesh around his big lips was jagged and there was a knot over his right eye that always looked red and raw.

In his years as a boxer Joppy had had moderate success. He was ranked number seven in 1932 but his big draw was the violence he brought to the ring. Joppy would come out swinging wildly, taking everything any boxer could dish out. In his prime no one could knock Joppy down and, later on, he always went the distance.

"He got something to do with the fights?" I asked.

"Wherever they's a little money to be made Mr. Albright got his nose to the ground," Joppy said. "An' he don't care too much if that money got a little smudge or sumpin' on it neither."

"So you got me tied up with a gangster?"

"Ain't no gangster, Ease. Mr. Albright just a man with a finger in a whole lotta pies, thas all. He's a businessman and you know when you in business sellin' shirts and a man come up to you with a box he say done falled off a truck, well . . . you just give that man a couple'a dollars and look t'other way." He waved his catcher's mitt at me. "Thas business."

Joppy was cleaning one area on his counter until it was spotless, except for the dirt that caked in the cracks. The dark cracks twisting through the light marble looked like a web of blood vessels in a newborn baby's head.

"So he's just a businessman?" I asked.

Joppy stopped wiping for a moment and looked me in the eye. "Don't get me wrong, Ease. DeWitt is a tough man, and he runs in bad company. But you still might could get that mortgage payment an' you might even learn sumpin' from'im."

I sat there looking around the small room. Joppy had six tables and seven high stools at his bar. A busy night never saw all his chairs full but I was jealous of his success. He had his own business; he owned something. He told me one night that he could sell that bar even though he only rented the room. I thought he was lying but later on I found out that people will buy a business that already has customers; they wouldn't mind paying the rent if there was money coming in.

The windows were dirty and the floor was rutted but it was Joppy's place and when the white butcher-boss came up to collect the rent he always said, "Thank you, Mr. Shag." Because he was happy to get his money.

"So what he want with me?" I asked.

"He just want you t'look for somebody, leastwise that what he said."

"Who?"

"Some girl, I dunno." Joppy shrugged. "I ain't ax him his business if it don't gotta do wit' me. But he just payin' you to *look,* ain't nobody says you gotta find nuthin'."

"And what's he gonna pay?"

"Enough fo' that mortgage. That's why I called you in on this, Easy, I know'd you need some fast money. I don't give a damn 'bout that man, or whoever it is he lookin' fo' neither."

The thought of paying my mortgage reminded me of my front yard and the shade of my fruit trees in the summer heat. I felt that I was just as good as any white man, but if I didn't even own my front door then people would look at me like just another poor beggar, with his hand outstretched.

"Take his money, man. You got to hold on to that little bit'a property," Joppy said as if he knew what I was thinking. "You know all them pretty girls you be runnin' wit' ain't gonna buy you no house."

"I don't like it, Joppy."

"You don't like that money? Shit! I'll hold it for ya."

"Not the money . . . It's just . . . You know that Mr. Albright reminds me of Mouse."

"Who?"

"You remember, he was a little man lived down in Houston. He married EttaMae Harris."

Joppy turned his jagged lips into a frown. "Naw, he must'a come after my time."

"Yeah, well, Mouse is a lot like Mr. Albright. He's smooth and a natty dresser and he's smilin' all the time. But he always got his business in the front'a his mind, and if you get in the way you might come to no good." I always tried to speak proper English in my life, the kind of English they taught in school, but I found over the years that I could only truly express myself in the natural, "uneducated" dialect of my upbringing.

" 'Might come to no good' is a bitch, Easy, but sleepin' in the street ain't got no 'might' to it."

"Yeah, man. I'm just feelin' kinda careful."

"Careful don't hurt, Easy. Careful keep your hands up, careful makes ya strong."

"So he's just a businessman, huh?" I asked again.

"Thas right!"

"And just exactly what kind of business is it he does? I mean, is he a shirt salesman or what?"

"They gotta sayin' for his line'a work, Ease."

"What's that?"

"Whatever the market can bear." He smiled, looking like a hungry bear himself. "Whatever the market can bear."

"I'll think about it."

"Don't worry, Ease, I'll take care'a ya. You just call ole Joppy now and then and I'll tell ya if it sounds like it's gettin' bad. You just keep in touch with me an' you be just fine."

"Thanks for thinkin'a me, Jop," I said, but I wondered if I'd still be thankful later on.

drove back to my house thinking about money and how much I needed to have some.

I loved going home. Maybe it was that I was raised on a share-cropper's farm or that I never owned anything until I bought that house, but I loved my little home. There was an apple tree and an avocado in the front yard, surrounded by thick St. Augustine grass. At the side of the house I had a pomegranate tree that bore more than thirty fruit every season and a banana tree that never produced a thing. There were dahlias and wild roses in beds around the fence and African violets that I kept in a big jar on the front porch.

The house itself was small. Just a living room, a bedroom, and a kitchen. The bathroom didn't even have a shower and the back yard was no larger than a child's rubber pool. But that house meant more to me than any woman I ever knew. I loved her and I was jealous of her and if the bank sent the county marshal to take her from me I might have come at him with a rifle rather than to give her up.

Working for Joppy's friend was the only way I saw to keep my house. But there was something wrong, I could feel it in my fingertips. DeWitt Albright made me uneasy; Joppy's tough words, though they were true, made me uneasy. I kept telling myself to go to bed and forget it.

"Easy," I said, "get a good night's sleep and go out looking for a job tomorrow."

"But this is June twenty-five," a voice said. "Where is the sixty-four dollars coming from on July one?"

"I'll get it," I answered.

"How?"

We went on like that but it was useless from the start. I knew I was going to take Albright's money and do whatever he wanted me to, providing it was legal, because that little house of mine needed me and I wasn't about to let her down.

And there was another thing.

DeWitt Albright made me a little nervous. He was a big man, and powerful by the look of him. You could tell by the way he held his shoulders that he was full of violence. But I was a big man too. And, like most young men, I never liked to admit that I could be dissuaded by fear.

Whether he knew it or not, DeWitt Albright had me caught by my own pride. The more I was afraid of him, I was that much more certain to take the job he offered.


The address Albright had given me was a small, buff-colored building on Alvarado. The buildings around it were taller but not as old or as distinguished. I walked through the black wrought-iron gates into the hall of the Spanish-styled entrance. There was nobody around, not even a directory, just a wall of cream-colored doors with no names on them.

"Excuse me."

The voice made me jump.

"What?" My voice strained and cracked as I turned to see the small man.

"Who are you looking for?"

He was a little white man wearing a suit that was also a uniform.

"I'm looking for, um . . . ah . . . ," I stuttered. I forgot the name. I had to squint so that the room wouldn't start spinning.

It was a habit I developed in Texas when I was a boy. Sometimes, when a white man of authority would catch me off guard, I'd empty my head of everything so I was unable to say anything. "The less you know, the less trouble you find," they used to say. I hated myself for it but I also hated white people, and colored people too, for making me that way.

"Can I help you?" the white man asked. He had curly red hair and a pointed nose. When I still couldn't answer he said, "We only take deliveries between nine and six."

"No, no," I said, trying to remember.

"Yes we do! Now you better leave."

"No, I mean I . . ."

The little man started backing toward a small podium that stood against the wall. I figured that he had a nightstick back there.

"Albright!" I yelled.

"What?" he yelled back.

"Albright! I'm here to see Albright!"

"Albright who?" There was suspicion in his eye, and his hand was behind the podium.

"Mr. Albright. Mr. DeWitt Albright."

"Mr. Albright?"

"Yes, that's him."

"Are you delivering something?" he asked, holding out his scrawny hand.

"No. I have an appointment. I mean, I'm supposed to meet him." I hated that little man.

"You're supposed to meet him? You can't even remember his name."

I took a deep breath and said, very softly, "I am supposed to meet Mr. DeWitt Albright tonight, any time after seven."

"You're supposed to meet him at seven? It's eight-thirty now. He's probably gone."

"He told me *any time* after seven."

He held out his hand to me again. "Did he give you a note saying you're to come in here after hours?"

I shook my head at him. I would have liked to rip the skin from his face like I'd done once to another white boy.

"Well, how am I to know that you aren't just a thief? You can't even remember his name and you want me to take you somewhere in there. Why you could have a partner waiting for me to let you in . . ."

I was disgusted. "Forget it man," I said. "You just tell him, when you see him, that Mr. Rawlins was here. You tell him that the next time he better give me a note because you cain't be lettin' no street niggahs comin' in yo' place wit' no notes!"

I was ready to leave. That little white man had convinced me that I was in the wrong place. I was ready to go back home. I could find my money another way.

"Hold on," he said. "You wait right there and I'll be back in a minute." He sidled through one of the cream-colored doors, shutting it as he went. I heard the lock snap into place a moment later.

After a few minutes he opened the door a crack and waved at me to follow him. He looked from side to side as he let me through the door; looking for my accomplices I suppose.

The doorway led to an open courtyard that was paved with dark red brick and landscaped with three large palm trees that reached out beyond the roof of the three-story building. The inner doorways on the upper two floors were enclosed by trellises that had vines of white and yellow sweetheart roses cascading down. The sky was still light at that time of year but I could see a crescent moon peeking over the inner roof.

The little man opened another door at the other side of the courtyard. It led down an ugly metal staircase into the bowels of the building. We went through a dusty boiler room to an empty corridor that was painted drab green and draped with gray cobwebs.

At the end of the hall there was a door of the same color that was chipped and dusty.

"That's what you want," the little man said.

I said thank you and he walked away from me. I never saw him again. I often think of how so many people have walked into my life for just a few minutes and kicked up some dust, then they're gone away. My father was like that; my mother wasn't much better.

I knocked on the ugly door. I expected to see Albright, but instead the door opened into a small room that held two strange-looking men.

The man who held the door was tall and slight with curly brown hair, dark skin like an India Indian, and brown eyes so light they were almost golden. His friend, who stood against a door at the far wall, was short and looked a little like he was Chinese around the eyes, but when I looked at him again I wasn't so sure of his race.

The dark man smiled and put out his hand. I thought he wanted to shake but then he started slapping my side.

"Hey, man! What's wrong with you?" I said, pushing him away. The maybe-Chinese man slipped a hand in his pocket.

"Mr. Rawlins," the dark man said in an accent I didn't know.

He was still smiling. "Put your hands up a little from your sides, please. I'm just checking." The smile widened into a grin.

"You could just keep your hands to yourself, man. I don't let nobody feel on me like that."

The little man pulled something, I couldn't tell what, halfway out of his pocket. Then he took a step toward us. The grinner tried to put his hand against my chest but I grabbed him by the wrist.

The dark man's eyes glittered, he smiled at me for a moment, and then said to his partner, "Don't worry, Manny. He's okay."

"You sure, Shariff?"

"Yeah. He's alright, just a little shaky." Shariff's teeth glinted between his dusky lips. I still had his wrist.

Shariff said, "Let him know, Manny."

Manny put his hand back in his pocket and then took it out again to knock on the door behind.

DeWitt Albright opened the door after a minute.

"Easy," he smiled.

"He doesn't want us to touch him," Shariff said as I let him go.

"Leave it," Albright answered. "I just wanted to make sure he was solo."

"You're the boss." Shariff sounded very sure of himself; even a little arrogant.

"You and Manny can go now," Albright smiled. "Easy and I have some business to talk over."


Mr. Albright went behind a big blond desk and put his bone shoes up next to a half-full bottle of Wild Turkey. There was a paper calendar hanging on the wall behind him with a picture of a basket of blackberries as a design. There was nothing else on the wall. The floor was bare too: plain yellow linoleum with flecks of color scattered through it.

"Have a seat, Mr. Rawlins," Mr. Albright said, gesturing to the chair in front of his desk. He was bare-headed and his coat was nowhere in sight. There was a white-leather shoulder holster under his left arm. The muzzle of the pistol almost reached his belt.

"Nice friends you got," I said as I studied his piece.

"They're like you, Easy. Whenever I need a little manpower I give them a call. There's a whole army of men who'll do specialized work for the right price."

"The little guy Chinese?"

Albright shrugged. "No one knows. He was raised in an orphanage, in Jersey City. Drink?"

"Sure."

"One of the benefits of working for yourself. Always have a bottle on the table. Everybody else, even the presidents of these big companies, got the booze in the bottom drawer, but I keep it right out in plain sight. You want to drink it? That's fine with me. You don't like it? Door's right there behind you." While he talked he poured two shots into glasses that he had taken from a desk drawer.

The gun interested me. The butt and the barrel were black; the only part of DeWitt's attire that wasn't white.

As I leaned over to take the glass from his hand he asked, "So, you want the job, Easy?"

"Well, that depends on what kind of job you had in mind?"

"I'm looking for somebody, for a friend," he said. He pulled a photograph from his shirt pocket and put it down on the desk. It was a picture of the head and shoulders of a pretty young white woman. The picture had been black and white originally but it was touched up for color like the photos of jazz singers that they put out in front of nightclubs. She had light hair coming down over her bare shoulders and high cheekbones and eyes that might have been blue if the artist got it right. After staring at her for a full minute I decided that she'd be worth looking for if you could get her to smile at you that way.

"Daphne Monet," Mr. Albright said. "Not bad to look at but she's hell to find."

"I still don't see what it's got to do with me," I said. "I ain't never laid eyes on her."

"That's a shame, Easy." He was smiling at me. "But I think you might be able to help me anyway."

"I can't see how. Woman like this don't hardly know my number. What you should do is call the police."

"I never call a soul who isn't a friend, or at least a friend of a friend. I don't know any cops, and neither do my friends."

"Well then get a—"

"You see, Easy," he cut me off, "Daphne has a predilection for the company of Negroes. She likes jazz and pigs' feet and dark meat, if you know what I mean."

I knew but I didn't like to hear it. "So you think she might be down around Watts?"

"Not a doubt in my mind. But, you see, I can't go in those places looking for her because I'm not the right persuasion. Joppy knows me well enough to tell me what he knows but I've already asked him and all he could do was to give me your name."

"So what do you want with her?"

"I have a friend who wants to apologize, Easy. He has a short temper and that's why she left."

"And he wants her back?"

Mr. Albright smiled.

"I don't know if I can help you, Mr. Albright. Like Joppy said, I lost a job a couple of days ago and I have to get another one before the note comes due."

"Hundred dollars for a week's work, Mr. Rawlins, and I pay in advance. You find her tomorrow and you keep what's in your pocket."

"I don't know, Mr. Albright. I mean, how do I know what I'm getting mixed up in? What are you—"

He raised a powerful finger to his lips, then he said, "Easy, walk out your door in the morning and you're mixed up in something. The only thing you can really worry about is if you get mixed up to the top or not."

"I don't want to get mixed up with the law is what I mean."

"That's why I want you to work for me. I don't like the police myself. Shit! The police enforce the law and you know what the law is, don't you?"

I had my own ideas on the subject but I kept them to myself.

"The law," he continued, "is made by the rich people so that the poor people can't get ahead. You don't want to get mixed up with the law and neither do I."

He lifted the shot glass and inspected it as if he were checking for fleas, then he put the glass on the desk and placed his hands, palms down, around it.

"I'm just asking you to find a girl," he said. "And to tell me where she is. That's all. You just find out where she is and whisper it in my ear. That's all. You find her and I'll give you a bonus mortgage payment and my friend will find you a job, maybe he can even get you back into Champion."

"Who is it wants to find the girl?"

"No names, Easy, it's better that way."

"It's just that I'd hate to find her and then have some cop come up to me with some shit like I was the last one seen around her— before she disappeared."

The white man laughed and shook his head as if I had told a good joke.

"Things happen every day, Easy," he said. "Things happen every day. You're an educated man, aren't you?"

"Why, yes."

"So you read the paper. You read it today?"

"Yes."

"Three murders! Three! Last night alone. Things happen every day. People with everything to live for, maybe they even got a little money in the bank. They probably had it all planned out what they'd be doing this weekend, but that didn't stop them from dying. Those plans didn't save them when the time came. People got everything to live for and they get a little careless. They forget that the only thing you have to be sure of is that nothing bad comes to you."

The way he smiled when he sat back in his chair reminded me of Mouse again. I thought of how Mouse was always smiling, especially when misfortune happened to someone else.

"You just find the girl and tell me, that's all. I'm not going to hurt her and neither is my friend. You don't have a thing to worry about."

He took a white secretary-type wallet from a desk drawer and produced a stack of bills. He counted out ten of them, licking his square thumb for every other one, and placed them in a neat stack next to the whiskey.

"One hundred dollars," he said.

I couldn't see why it shouldn't be my one hundred dollars.


When I was a poor man, and landless, all I worried about was a place for the night and food to eat; you really didn't need much for that. A friend would always stand me a meal, and there were plenty of women who would have let me sleep with them. But when I got that mortgage I found that I needed more than just friendship. Mr. Albright wasn't a friend but he had what I needed.

He was a fine host too. His liquor was good and he was pleasant enough. He told me a few stories, the kind of tales that we called "lies" back home in Texas.

One story he told was about when he was a lawyer in Georgia.

"I was defending a shit-kicker who was charged with burning down a banker's house," DeWitt told me as he stared out toward the wall behind my head. "Banker had foreclosed on the boy the minute the note was due. You know he didn't even give him any chance to make extra arrangements. And that boy was just as guilty as that banker was."

"You get him off?" I asked.

DeWitt smiled at me. "Yeah. That prosecutor had a good case on Leon, that's the shit-kicker. Yeah, the honorable Randolph Corey had solid proof that my client did the arson. But I went down to Randy's house and I sat at his table and pulled out this here pistol. All I did was talk about the weather we'd been having, and while I did that I cleaned my gun."

"Getting your client off meant that much to you?"

"Shit. Leon was trash. But Randy had been riding pretty high for a couple'a years and I had it in mind that it was time for him to lose a case." Albright straightened his shoulders. "You have to have a sense of balance when it comes to the law, Easy. Everything has to come out just right."

After a few drinks I started talking about the war. Plain old man-talk, about half of it true and the rest just for laughs. More than an hour went by before he asked me, "You ever kill a man with your hands, Easy?"

"What?"

"You ever kill a man, hand-to-hand?"

"Why?"

"No reason really. It's just that I know you've seen some action."

"Some."

"You ever kill somebody up close? I mean so close that you could see it when his eyes went out of focus and he let go? When you kill a man it's the shit and piss that's worst. You boys did that in the war and I bet it was bad. I bet you couldn't dream about your mother anymore, or anything nice. But you lived with it because you knew that it was the war that forced you to do it."

His pale blue eyes reminded me of the wide-eyed corpses of German soldiers that I once saw stacked up on a road to Berlin.

"But the only thing that you have to remember, Easy," he said as he picked up the money to hand me across the table, "is that some of us can kill with no more trouble than drinking a glass of bourbon." He downed the shot and smiled.

Then he said, "Joppy tells me that you used to frequent an illegal club down on Eighty-ninth and Central. Somebody saw Daphne at that very same bar not long ago. I don't know what they call it but they have the big names in there on weekends and the man who runs it is called John. You could start tonight."

The way his dead eyes shined on me I knew our party was over. I couldn't think of anything to say so I nodded, put his money in my pocket, and moved to leave.

I turned back at the door to salute him goodbye but DeWitt Albright had filled his glass and shifted his gaze to the far wall. He was staring into someplace far from that dirty basement.

**J**ohn's place was a speakeasy before they repealed Prohibition. But by 1948 we had legitimate bars all over L.A. John liked the speakeasy business though, and he had been in so much trouble with the law that City Hall wouldn't have given him a license to drive, much less to sell liquor. So John kept paying off the police and running an illegal nightclub through the back door of a little market at the corner of Central Avenue and Eighty-ninth Place. You could walk into that store any evening up until three in the morning to find Hattie Parsons sitting behind the candy counter. They didn't have many groceries, and no fresh produce or dairy goods, but she'd sell you what was there and if you knew the right words, or were a regular, then she'd let you in the club through the back door. But if you thought that you should be able to get in on account of your name, or your clothes or maybe your bankbook, well, Hattie kept a straight razor in her apron pocket and her nephew, Junior Fornay, sat right behind the door.

When I pushed open the door to the market I ran into my third white man that day. This one was about my height with wheat-brown hair and an expensive dark blue suit. His clothes were disheveled, and he smelled of gin.

"Hey, colored brother," he said as he waved at me. He walked straight toward me so that I had to back out of the store if I didn't want him to run me down.

"How'd ya like t'make twenty dollars fast?" he asked when the door swung shut behind him.

They were just throwing money at me that day.

"How's that?" I asked the drunk.

"I need to get in here . . . lookin' fer someone. Girl in there won't let me in." He was teetering and I was afraid he'd fall down. "Why'ont you tell'em I'm fine."

"I'm sorry, but I can't do that," I said.

"Why's that?"

"Once they tell you no at John's they stick to it." I moved around him to get into the door again. He tried to turn and grab my arm but all he managed was to spin around twice and wind up sitting against the wall. He put up his hand as if he wanted me to bend down so he could whisper something but I didn't think that anything he had to offer could improve my life.

"Hey, Hattie," I said. "Looks like you got a boarder out on your doorstep."

"Drunk ole white boy?"

"Yep."

"I'll have Junior look out there later on. He can sweep'im up if he still there."

With that I put the drunk out of my mind. "Who you got playin' tonight?" I asked.

"Some'a your homefolks, Easy. Lips and his trio. But we had Holiday, Tuesday last."

"You did?"

"She just come breezin' through." Hattie's smile revealed teeth that were like flat gray pebbles. "Must'a been 'bout, I don't know, midnight, but the birds was singin' wit'er 'fore we closed for the night."

"Oh man! Sorry I missed that," I said.

"That'a be six bits, baby."

"What for?"

"John put on a cover. Cost goin' up an' he tryin' t'keep out the riff-raff."

"And who's that?"

She leaned forward showing me her watery brown eyes. Hattie was the color of light sand and I doubt if she ever topped a hundred pounds in her sixty-some years.

"You heard about Howard?" she asked.

"What Howard?"

"Howard Green, the chauffeur."

"No, uh-uh. I haven't seen Howard Green since last Christmas."

"Well you ain't gonna see him no more—in this world."

"What happened?"

"He walked outta here about three in the mo'nin' the night Lady Day was here and wham!" She slammed her bony fist into an open palm.

"Yeah?"

"They din't hardly even leave a face on'im. You know I tole'im that he was a fool t'be walkin' out on Holiday but he didn't care. Said he had *business* t'see to. Hmm! I tole him he hadn't oughtta left."

"Killed him?"

"Right out there next to his car. Beat him so bad that his wife, Esther, said the only way she could identify the body was cuz of his ring. They must'a used a lead pipe. You know he had his nose in somebody's nevermind."

"Howard liked to play hard," I agreed. I handed her three quarters.

"Go right on in, honey," she smiled.


When I opened the door I was slapped in the face by the force of Lips' alto horn. I had been hearing Lips and Willie and Flattop since I was a boy in Houston. All of them and John and half the people in that crowded room had migrated from Houston after the war, and some before that. California was like heaven for the southern Negro. People told stories of how you could eat fruit right off the trees and get enough work to retire one day. The stories were true for the most part but the truth wasn't like the dream. Life was still hard in L.A. and if you worked every day you still found yourself on the bottom.

But being on the bottom didn't feel so bad if you could come to John's now and then and remember how it felt back home in Texas, dreaming about California. Sitting there and drinking John's scotch you could remember the dreams you once had and, for a while, it felt like you had them for real.

"Hey, Ease," a thick voice crackled at me from behind the door.

It was Junior Fornay. He was a man that I knew from back home too. A big, burly field hand who could chop cotton all day long and then party until it was time to climb back out into the fields. We had had an argument once, when we were both much younger, and I couldn't help thinking that I'd've probably died if it wasn't for Mouse stepping in to save my bacon.

"Junior," I hailed. "What's goin' on?"

"Not too much, yet, but stick around." He was leaning back on a stool, propping himself against the wall. He was five years older than I, maybe thirty-three, and his gut hung over his jeans, but Junior still looked to be every bit as powerful as when he put me on the floor all those years before.

Junior had a cigarette between his lips. He smoked the cheapest, foulest brand that they made in Mexico—Zapatas. I guess that he was finished smoking it because he let it fall to the floor. It just lay on the oak floor, smoldering and burning a black patch in the wood. The floor around Junior's chair had dozens of burns in it. He was a filthy man who didn't give a damn about anything.

"Ain't seen ya 'round much, Ease. Where ya been?"

"Workin', workin', day and night for Champion, and then they let me go."

"Fired?" There was a hint of a smile on his lips.

"On my ass."

"Shit. Sorry t'hear it. They got layoffs?"

"Naw, man. It's just that the boss ain't happy if you just do your job. He need a big smack on his butt too."

"I hear ya."

"Just this past Monday I finished a shift and I was so tired I couldn't even walk straight . . ."

"Uh-huh," Junior chimed in to keep the story going.

". . . and the boss come up and say that he need me for an extra hour. Well I told him that I was sorry but I had a date. And I did too, with my bed."

Junior got a kick out of that.

"And he got the nerve to tell me that *my people* have to learn to give a little extra if we wanna advance."

"He said that?"

"Yeah." I felt the heat of my anger returning.

"And what is he?"

"Italian boy, I think his parents the ones come over."

"Man! So what you say?"

"I told him that my people been givin' a little extra since before

Italy was even a country. 'Cause you know Italy ain't even been around that long."

"Yeah," Junior said. But I could see that he didn't know what I was talking about. "So what happened then?"

"He just told me to go on home and not to bother coming back. He said that he needed people who were willing to work. So I left."

"Man!" Junior shook his head. "They do it to ya every time."

"That's right. You want a beer, Junior?"

"Yeah." He frowned. "But can you buy it with no job and all?"

"I can always buy a couple'a beers."

"Well then, I can always drink'em."

I went over to the bar and ordered two ales. It looked like half of Houston was there. Most tables had five or six people. People were shouting and talking, kissing and laughing. John's place felt good after a hard day's work. It wasn't quite legal but there was nothing wrong with it either. Big names in Negro music came there because they knew John in the old days when he gave them work and didn't skimp on the paycheck. There must've been over two hundred regulars that frequented John's and we all knew each other, so it made a good place for business as well as a good time.

Alphonso Jenkins was there in his black silk shirt and his foot-high pompadour hairdo. Jockamo Johanas was there too. He was wearing a wooly brown suit and bright blue shoes. Skinny Rita Cook was there with five men hanging around her table. I never did understand how an ugly, skinny woman like that attracted so many men. I once asked her how she did it and she said, in her high whiny voice, "Well, ya know, Easy, it's only half the mens is int'rested in how a girl look. Most'a your colored mens is lookin' for a woman love'em so hard that they fo'gets how hard it is t'make it through the day."

I noticed Frank Green at the bar. We called him Knifehand because he was so fast to pull a knife that it seemed he always had one in his hand. I stayed away from Frank because he was a gangster. He hijacked liquor trucks and cigarette shipments all over California, and Nevada too. He was serious about everything and just about ready to cut any man he met.

I noted that Frank was wearing all dark clothes. In Frank's line of business that meant he was about to go out to work—hijacking or worse.

The room was so crowded that there was barely any space to dance, but there were a dozen or so couples wrestling out there between the tables.

I carried the two mugs of ale back to the entrance and handed Junior his. One of the few ways I know to make a foul-tempered field hand happy is to feed him some ale and let him tell a few tall tales. So I sat back and sipped while Junior told me about the goings-on at John's for the previous week or so. He told me the story about Howard Green again. When he told it he added that Green had been doing some illegal work for his employers and, Junior thought, "It's them white men kilt'im."

Junior liked to make up any old wild story, I knew that, but there were too many white people turning up for me to feel at ease.

"Who was he workin' for?" I asked.

"You know that dude dropped outta the mayor's race?"

"Matthew Teran?"

Teran had a good chance at winning the mayor's race in L.A. but he'd just withdrawn his name a few weeks before. Nobody knew why.

"Yeah, that's him. You know all them politicians is just robbers. Why I remember when they first elected Huey Long, down in Louisiana—"

"How long Lips gonna be here?" I asked, to cut him off.

"Week or so." Junior didn't care what he talked about. "They bring back some mem'ries, don't they. Shit, they was playin' that night Mouse pulled me off your ass."

"Thas right," I said. I can still feel Junior's foot in my kidney when I turn the wrong way.

"I should'a thanked'im for that. You know I was so drunk an' so mad that I might'a kilt you, Easy. And then I'd still be on the chain gang."

That was the first real smile he showed since I'd been with him. Junior was missing two teeth from the lower row and one upper.

"What ever happened to Mouse?" he asked, almost wistfully.

"I don't know. Today's the first time I even thought about him in years."

"He still down there in Houston?"

"Last I heard. He married to EttaMae."

"What's he doin' when you seen'im last?"

"Been so long I don't even remember," I lied.

Junior grinned. "I remember when he killed Joe T., you know the pimp? I mean Joe had blood comin' from everywhere an' Mouse had on this light blue suit. Not a spot on it! You know that's why the cops didn't take Mouse in, they didn't even think he could'a done it 'cause he was too clean."

I was remembering the last time I had seen Raymond Alexander, and it wasn't something to make me laugh.


I hadn't seen Mouse in four years when we ran into each other one night, outside of Myrtle's saloon, in Houston's Fifth Ward. He was wearing a plum-colored suit and a felt brown derby. I was still wearing army green.

" 'S'appenin', Easy?" he asked, looking up at me. Mouse was a small, rodent-faced man.

"Not much," I answered. "You look jus' 'bout the same."

Mouse flashed his gold-rimmed teeth at me. "Ain't so bad. I got the streets tame by now."

We smiled at each other and slapped backs. Mouse bought me a drink in Myrtle's and I bought him another. We traded back and forth like that until Myrtle locked us in and went up to bed. She said, "Leave the money fo' what you'all drink under the counter. Do' lock itself on the way out."

" 'Member that shit wit' my stepdaddy, Ease?" Mouse asked when we were alone.

"Yeah," I said softly. It was early morning and empty in the bar but I still looked around the room; murder should never be discussed out loud, but Mouse didn't know it. He had killed his stepfather five years earlier and blamed it on another man. But if the law ever found out the true circumstances he'd have been hanging in a week.

"His real son, Navrochet, come lookin' fo' me last year. He din't think that boy Clifton done it even though the law said he did." Mouse poured a drink and knocked it back. Then he poured another one. "You get any white pussy in the war?" he asked.

"All they got is white girls. What you think?"

Mouse grinned and sat back, rubbing his crotch. "Shit!" he said. "that might be worf a couple'a potshots, huh?" And he slapped my knee like in the old days when we were partners, before the war.

We were drinking for an hour before he got back to Navrochet. Mouse said, "Man come down here, right in this saloon, and come up on me wit' his high boots on. You know I had t'look straight up t'see that boy. He had on a nice suit wit' them boots, so I jus' slipped down my zipper when he walk in. He say he wanna talk. He say les step outside. And I go. You might call me a fool but I go. And the minute I get out there and turn around he got a pistol pointed at my fo'head. Can you imagine that? So I play like I'm scared. Then ole Navro wanna know where he could fine you . . ."

"Me!" I said.

"Yeah, Easy! He heard you was wit' me so he gonna kill you

too. But I'as workin' my stomach in and out and you know I had
some beer in me. I'as actin' like I'as scared and had Navro thinkin' he so bad 'cause I'm shakin' . . . Then I pulls out Peter and
open up the dam. Heh, heh. Piss all over his boots. You know
Navrochet like t'jump three feet." The grin faded from his lips
and he said, "I shot him four times 'fore he hit the floor. Same
amount'a lead I put in his fuckin' son-of-a-whore daddy."

I had seen a lot of death in the war but Navrochet's dying
seemed more real and more terrible; it was so useless. Back in
Texas, in Fifth Ward, Houston, men would kill over a dime wager
or a rash word. And it was always the evil ones that would kill the
good or the stupid. If anyone should have died in that bar it
should have been Mouse. If there was any kind of justice he
should have been the one.

"He caught me one in the chest though, Ease," Mouse said, as
if he could read my mind. "You know I was layin' up against the
wall wit' no feelin' in my arms or legs. Everything was kinda fuzzy
an' I hear this voice and I see this white face over me." He
sounded almost like a prayer. "And that white face told me that
he was death an' wasn't I scared. And you know what I told him?"

"What?" I asked, and at that same moment I resolved to leave
Texas forever.

"I tole'im that I had a man beat me four ways from sundown my
whole life and I sent him t'hell. I say, 'I sent his son after'im, so
Satan stay wit' me and I whip yo' ass too.'"

Mouse laughed softly, laid his head on the bar, and went to
sleep. I pulled out my wallet, quietly as if I were afraid to waken
the dead, left two bills, and went down to the hotel. I was on a bus
for Los Angeles before the sun came up.


But it seemed like a lifetime had passed since then. I was a land-
owner that night and I was working for my mortgage.

"Junior," I said. "Many white girls been in here lately?"

"Why? You lookin' fo' one?" Junior was naturally suspicious.

"Well . . . kinda."

"You kinda lookin' fo' one! When you gonna find out?"

"You see, uh, I heard about this girl. Um . . . Delia or Dahlia or sumpin'. I know it starts with a 'D.' Anyway she has blond hair and blue eyes and I been told that she was worth lookin' at."

"Cain't say I remember, man. I mean some white girls come in on the weekends, you know, but they don't never come alone. And I lose my job wolfin' after some other brother's date."

I had the notion that Junior was lying to me. Even if he knew the answer to my question he would have kept it quiet. Junior hated anybody who he thought was doing better than he was. Junior hated everybody.

"Yeah, well, I guess I'll see her if she comes in." I looked around the room. "There's a chair over there next to the band, think I'll grab it."

I knew Junior was watching me as I left him but I didn't care. He wouldn't help me and I didn't give a damn about him.

I found a chair next to my friend Odell Jones.

Odell was a quiet man and a religious man. His head was the color and shape of a red pecan. And even though he was a God-fearing man he'd find his way down to John's about three or four times a week. He'd sit there until midnight nursing a bottle of beer, not saying a word unless somebody spoke to him.

Odell was soaking up all the excitement so he could carry it around with him on his job as a janitor at the Pleasant Street school. Odell always wore an old gray tweed jacket and thread-bare brown woolen pants.

"Hey, Odell," I greeted him.

"Easy."

"How's it going tonight?"

"Well," he said slowly, thinking it over. "It's goin' alright. It sure is goin'."

I laughed and slapped Odell on the shoulder. He was so slight that the force pushed him to the side but he just smiled and sat back up. Odell was older than most of my friends by twenty years or more; I think he was almost fifty then. To this day he's outlived two wives and three out of four children.

"What's it look like tonight, Odell?"

" 'Bout two hours ago," he said while he scratched his left ear, "Fat Wilma Johnson come in with Toupelo and danced up a storm. She jump up in the air and come down so hard this whole room like t'shook."

"That Wilma like to dance," I said.

"Don't know how she keep that much heft, hard as she work and hard as she play."

"She probably eat hard too."

That tickled Odell.

I asked him to hold a seat for me while I went around saying hello.

I made the rounds shaking hands and asking people if they had seen a white girl, Delia or Dahlia or something. I didn't use her real name because I didn't want anybody to connect me with her if Mr. Albright turned out to be wrong and there was trouble. But no one had seen her. I would have even asked Frank Green but he was gone by the time I worked my way to the bar.

When I got back to my table Odell was still there and smiling.

"Hilda Redd come in," he said to me.

"Yeah?"

"Lloyd try to make a little time an' she hit him in that fat gut so hard he a'most went down." Odell acted out Lloyd's part, puffing his cheeks and bulging his eyes.

We were still laughing when I heard a shout that was so loud even Lips looked up from his horn.

"Easy!"

Odell looked up.

"Easy Rawlins, is that you?"

A big man walked into the room. A big man in a white suit with blue pinstripes and a ten-gallon hat. A big black man with a wide white grin who moved across the crowded room like a cloud-burst, raining hellos and howyadoin's on the people he passed as he waded to our little table.

"Easy!" he laughed. "You ain't jumped outta no windahs yet?"

"Not yet, Dupree."

"You know Coretta, right?"

I noticed her there behind Dupree; he had her in tow like a child's toy wagon.

"Hi, Easy," she said in a soft voice.

"Hey, Coretta, how are ya?"

"Fine," she said quietly. She spoke so softly that I was surprised I understood her over the music and the noise. Maybe I really didn't hear her at all but just understood what she meant by the way she looked at me and the way she smiled.

Dupree and Coretta were as different as any two people could be. He was muscular and had an inch or two on me, maybe six-two, and he was loud and friendly as a big dog. Dupree was a smart man as far as books and numbers went but he was always broke because he'd squander his money on liquor and women, and if there was any left over you could talk him out of it with any old hard-luck story.

But Coretta was something else altogether. She was short and round with cherry-brown skin and big freckles. She always wore dresses that accented her bosom. Coretta was sloe-eyed. Her gaze moved from one part of the room to another almost aim-lessly, but you still had the feeling that she was watching you. She was a vain man's dream.

"Miss ya down at the plant, Ease," Dupree said. "Yeah, it just ain't the same wit'out you down there t'keep me straight. Them other niggahs just cain't keep up."

"I guess you have to do without me from now on, Dupree."

"Uh-uh, no. I cain't live with that. Benny wants you back, Easy. He's sorry he let you go."

"First I heard of it."

"You know them I-talians, Ease, they cain't say they sorry 'cause it's a shame to'em. But he wants you back though, I know that."

"Could we sit down with you and Odell, Easy?" Coretta said sweetly.

"Sure, sure. Get her a chair, Dupree. Com'on pull up here between us, Coretta."

I called the bartender to send over a quart of bourbon and a pail of chipped ice.

"So he wants me back, huh?" I asked Dupree once we all had a glass.

"Yeah! He told me this very day that if you walked in that door he'd take you back in a minute."

"First he want me to kiss his be-hind," I said. I noticed that Coretta's glass was already empty. "You want me to freshen that, Coretta?"

"Maybe I'll have another lil taste, if you wanna pour." I could feel her smile all the way down my spine.

Dupree said, "Shoot, Easy, I told him that you was sorry 'bout what happened an' he's willin' t'let it pass."

"I'm a sorry man alright. Any man without his paycheck is sorry."

Dupree's laugh was so loud that he almost knocked poor Odell over with the volume. "Well see, there you go!" Dupree bellowed. "You come on down on Friday an' we got yo' job back for sure."

I asked them about the girl too, but it was no use.

At midnight, exactly, Odell stood up to leave. He said good-night to Dupree and me, then he kissed Coretta's hand. She even kindled a fire under that quiet little man.

Then Dupree and I settled in to tell lies about the war. Coretta laughed and put away whiskey. Lips and his trio played on. People came in and out of the bar all night but I had given up on Miss Daphne Monet for the evening. I figured that if I got my job back at the plant I could return Mr. Albright's money. Anyway, the whiskey made me lazy—all I wanted to do was laugh.

Dupree passed out before we finished the second quart; that was about 3 A.M.

Coretta twisted up her nose at the back of his head and said, "He use' to play till the cock crowed, but that ole cock don't crow nearly so much no mo'."

**6**

"They done throwed him outta his place cuz he missed the rent," Coretta said.

We were dragging Dupree from the car to her door; his feet trailed two deep furrows in the landlord's lawn.

She went on to say, "First-class machinist at almost five dollars a hour but he cain't even pay his bills."

I couldn't help thinking that she wouldn't have been so put out if Dupree held his liquor a little better.

"Throw'im in there on the bed, Easy," she said after we got him through the front door.

Dupree was a big man and he was lucky that I could pile him in the bed at all. By the time I was through pulling and pushing his dead weight I was exhausted. I stumbled from Coretta's tiny bedroom to her even smaller living room.

She poured me a little nightcap and we sat on her sofa. We sat close to each other because her room wasn't much larger than a broom closet. And if I said something halfway funny she'd laugh and rock until she bent down to clutch my knee for a moment and then she'd look up to shine her hazel eyes on me. We spoke softly and Dupree's deep snoring drowned out a good half of whatever we said. Every time Coretta had something to say she whispered it in a confidential way and shifted a little closer to me, to make sure I heard her.

When we were so close that we were passing the same breath back and forth between us, I said, "I better be goin', Coretta. Sun catch me tiptoein' out your door and no tellin' what your neighbors say."

"Hmm! Dupree fall asleep on me an' you jus' gonna turn your back, walk out the door like I was dog food."

"You got another man right in the next room, baby. What if he hears sumpin'?"

"Way he snorin'?" She slid her hand into her blouse, lifting the bodice to air her breasts.

I staggered to my feet and took the two steps to the door.

"You be sorry if you go, Ease."

"I be more sorry if I stay," I said.

She didn't say anything to that. She just laid back on the sofa, fanning her bosom.

"I gotta go," I said. I even opened the door.

"Daphne be 'sleep now," Coretta smiled, and popped open a button. "You cain't get none'a that right now."

"What you call her?"

"Daphne. Ain't that right? You said Delia but that ain't her real name. We got real tight last week when her date an' my date was at the Playroom."

"Dupree?"

"Naw, Easy, it was somebody else. You know I never got just one boyfriend."

Coretta got up and walked right into my arms. I could smell the scent of cool jasmine coming in through the screen door and hot jasmine rising from her breast.

I had been old enough to kill men in a war but I wasn't a man yet. At least I wasn't a man the way Coretta was a woman. She straddled me on the couch and whispered, "Oh yeah, daddy, you hittin' my spot! Oh yeah, yeah!" It was all I could do not to yell. Then she jumped off of me saying, in a shy voice, "Oooo, that's jus' *too* good, Easy." I tried to pull her back but Coretta never went where she didn't want to go. She just twisted down to the floor and said, "I cain't get up off'a that much love, daddy, not the way things is."

"What things?" I cried.

"You know." She gestured with a twist of her head. "Dupree's right there in the next room."

"Fo'get about him! You got me goin', Coretta."

"It just ain't right, Easy. Here I am doin' this right in the next room and all you doin' is nosin' after my friend Daphne."

"I ain't after her, honey. It's just a job, that's all."

"What job?"

"Man wants me to find her."

"What man?"

"Who cares what man? I ain't nosin' after nobody but you."

"But Daphne's my friend . . ."

"Just some boyfriend, Coretta, that's all."

When I started to lose my excitement she gave me her spot again and let me hit it some more. In that way she kept me talking until the sky turned light. She *did* tell me who Daphne's boyfriend was; I wasn't happy to hear it, but it was better that I knew.

When Dupree started coughing like a man about to wake up I hustled on my pants and made to leave. Coretta hugged me around the chest and sighed, "Don't ole Coretta get a little ten dollars if you fines that girl, Easy? I *was* the one said about it."

"Sure, baby," I said. "Soon as I get it." When she kissed me goodbye I could tell the night was over: Her kiss would have hardly roused a dead man.

**W**hen I finally made it back to my house, on 116th Street, it was another beautiful California day. Big white clouds sailed eastward toward the San Bernadino mountain range. There were still traces of snow on the peaks and there was the lingering scent of burning trash in the air.

My studio couch was in the same position it had been in the morning before. The paper I'd been reading that morning was still folded neatly on my upholstered chair. The breakfast plates were in the sink.

I opened the blinds and picked up the stack of mail the mailman had dropped through the door slot. Once I'd become a homeowner I got mail every day—and I loved it. I even loved junk mail.

There was a letter promising me a free year of insurance and one where I stood a chance of winning a thousand dollars. There was a chain letter that prophesied my death if I didn't send six exact copies to other people I knew and two silver dimes to a post office box in Illinois. I supposed that it was a white gang preying on the superstition of southern Negros. I just threw that letter away.

But, on the whole, it was pretty nice sitting there in the slatted morning light and reading my mail. The electric percolator was making sounds from the kitchen and birds were chirping outside.

I turned over a big red packet full of coupons to show a tiny blue envelope underneath. It smelled of perfume and was written in a fancy woman's hand. It was postmarked from Houston and the name over the address read "Mr. Ezekiel Rawlins." That got me to move to the light of the kitchen window. It wasn't every day that I got a letter from home, by someone who knew my given name.

I looked out of the window for a moment before I read the letter. There was a jay looking down from the fence at the evil dog in the yard behind mine. The mongrel was growling and jumping at the bird. Every time he slammed his body against the wire fence the jay started as if he were about to fly off, but he didn't. He just kept staring down into those deadly jaws, mesmerized by the spectacle there.

Hey Easy!

Been a dog's age brother. Sophie give me your address. She come back down to Houston cause she say it's too much up there in Hollywood. Man, you know I asked her what she mean by too much but she just say, "Too much!" And you know every time I hear that I get a kind of chill like maybe too much is just right for me.

Everybody down here is the same. They tore down the Claxton Street Lodge. You should have seen the rats they had under that place!

Etta's good but she throwed me out. I come back from Lucinda's one night so drunk that I didn't even wash up. I sure am sorry about that. You know you gotta respect your woman, and a shower ain't too much to ask. But I guess she'll take me back one day.

You gotta see our boy, Easy. LaMarque is beautiful. You should see how big he is already! Etta says that he's lucky not to have my ratty look. But you know I think I see a little twinkle in his eye though. Anyway, he got big feet and a big mouth so I know he's doing okay.

I been thinking that maybe we ain't seen each other in too long, Ease. I been thinking maybe now I'm a bachelor again that maybe I could come visit and we burn down the town.

Why don't you write me and tell me when's a good time. You can send the letter to Etta, she see that I get it.

*See you soon,*

P.S.
I got Lucinda writing this letter for me and I told her that if she don't write down every word like I say then I'm a beat her butt down Avenue B so hold onto it, alright?

At the first words I went to my closet. I don't know what I wanted to do there, maybe pack my bags and leave town. Maybe I just wanted to hide in the closet, I don't know.

When we were young men, in Texas, we were the best of friends. We fought in the streets side by side and we shared the same women without ever getting mad about it. What was a woman compared to the love of two friends? But when it came time for Mouse to marry EttaMae Harris things began to change.

He came to my house late one night and got me to drive him, in a stolen car, down to a little farming town called Pariah. He said that he was going to ask his stepfather for an inheritance his mother had promised him before she died.

Before we left that town Mouse's stepfather and a young man named Clifton had been shot dead. When I drove Mouse back to Houston he had more than a thousand dollars in his pocket.

I had nothing to do with those shootings. But Mouse told me what he did on the drive back home. He told me that he and Clifton held up daddy Reese because the old man wouldn't relent to Mouse's claim. He told me that when Reese got to a gun Clifton was cut down, and then Mouse killed Reese. He said all that in complete innocence as he counted out three hundred dollars, blood money, for me.

Mouse didn't ever feel bad about anything he'd done. He was just that kind of man. He wasn't confessing to me, he was telling his story. There was nothing he ever did in his life that he didn't tell at least one person. And once he told me he gave me three hundred dollars so he would know I thought he had done right.

It was the worst thing I ever did to take that money. But my best friend would have put a bullet in my head if he ever thought that I was unsure of him. He would have seen me as an enemy, killed me for my lack of faith.

I ran away from Mouse and Texas to go to the army and then later to L.A. I hated myself. I signed up to fight in the war to prove to myself that I was a man. Before we launched the attack on D-Day I was frightened but I fought. I fought despite the fear. The first time I fought a German hand-to-hand I screamed for help the whole time I was killing him. His dead eyes stared at me a full five minutes before I let go of his throat.

The only time in my life that I had ever been completely free from fear was when I ran with Mouse. He was so confident that there was no room for fear. Mouse was barely five-foot-six but he'd go up against a man Dupree's size and you know I'd bet on the Mouse to walk away from it. He could put a knife in a man's stomach and ten minutes later sit down to a plate of spaghetti.

I didn't want to write Mouse and I didn't want to let it lie. In my mind he had such power that I felt I had to do whatever he wanted. But I had dreams that didn't have me running in the streets anymore; I was a man of property and I wanted to leave my wild days behind.

I drove down to the liquor store and bought a fifth of vodka and a gallon of grapefruit soda. I positioned myself in a chair at the front window and watched the day pass.

Looking out of the window is different in Los Angeles than it is in Houston. No matter where you live in a southern city (even a wild and violent place like Fifth Ward, Houston) you see almost everybody you know by just looking out your window. Every day is a parade of relatives and old friends and lovers you once had, and maybe you'd be lovers again one day.

That's why Sophie Anderson went back home I suppose. She liked the slower life of the South. When she looked out her window she wanted to see her friends and her family. And if she called out to one of them she wanted to know that they'd have the time to stop for a while and say hello.

Sophie was a real Southerner, so much so that she could never last in the workaday world of Los Angeles.

Because in L.A. people don't have time to stop; anywhere they have to go they go there in a car. The poorest man has a car in Los Angeles; he might not have a roof over his head but he has a car. And he knows where he's going too. In Houston and Galveston, and way down in Louisiana, life was a little more aimless. People worked a little job but they couldn't make any real money no matter what they did. But in Los Angeles you could make a hundred dollars in a week if you pushed. The promise of getting rich pushed people to work two jobs in the week and do a little plumbing on the weekend. There's no time to walk down the street or make a bar-b-q when somebody's going to pay you real money to haul refrigerators.

So I watched empty streets that day. Every once in a while I'd see a couple of children on bicycles or a group of young girls going to the store for candy and soda pop. I sipped vodka and napped and reread Mouse's letter until I knew that there was nothing I could do. I decided to ignore it and if he ever asked I'd just look simple and act like it never got delivered.

By the time the sun went down I was at peace with myself. I had a name, an address, a hundred dollars, and the next day I'd go ask for my old job back. I had a house and an empty bottle of vodka that had made me feel good.

The letter was postmarked two weeks earlier. If I was very lucky Etta had already taken Mouse back in.


When the telephone woke me it was black outside.

"Hello?"

"Mr. Rawlins, I've been expecting your call."

That threw me. I said, "What?"

"I hope you have some good news for me."

"Mr. Albright, is that you?"

"Sure is, Easy. What's shaking?"

It took me another moment to compose myself. I had planned to call him in a few days so it would seem like I had worked for his money.

"I got what you want," I said, in spite of my plans. "She's with—"

"Hold on to that, Easy. I like to look a man in the face when we do business. Telephone's no place for business. Anyway, I can't give you your bonus on the phone."

"I can come down to your office in the morning."

"Why don't we get together now? You know where the merry-go-round is down at Santa Monica pier?"

"Well, yeah, but . . ."

"That's about halfway between us. Why don't we meet there?"

"But what time is it?"

"About nine. They close the ride in an hour so we can be alone."

"I don't know . . . I just got up . . ."

"I *am* paying you."

"Okay. I'll get down there soon as I can drive it."

He hung up in my ear.

There was still a large stretch of farmland between Los Angeles and Santa Monica in those days. The Japanese farmers grew artichokes, lettuce, and strawberries along the sides of the road. That night the fields were dark under the slight moon and the air was chill but not cold.

I was unhappy about going to meet Mr. Albright because I wasn't used to going into white communities, like Santa Monica, to conduct business. The plant I worked at, Champion Aircraft, was in Santa Monica but I'd drive out there in the daytime, do my work, and go home. I never loitered anywhere except among my own people, in my own neighborhood.

But the idea that I'd give him the information he wanted, and that he'd give me enough money to pay the next month's mortgage, made me happy. I was dreaming about the day I'd be able to buy more houses, maybe even a duplex. I always wanted to own enough land that it would pay for itself out of the rent it generated.

When I arrived the merry-go-round and arcade were closing down. Small children and their parents were leaving and a group of young people were milling around, smoking cigarettes and acting tough the way young people do.

I went across the pier to the railing that looked down onto the beach. I figured that Mr. Albright would see me there as well as any place and that I was far enough away from the white kids that I could avoid any ugliness.

But that wasn't my week for avoiding anything bad.

A chubby girl in a tight-fitting skirt wandered away from her friends. She was younger than the rest of them, maybe seventeen, and it seemed like she was the only girl without a date. When she saw me she smiled and said, "Hi." I answered and turned away to look out over the weakly lit shoreline north of Santa Monica. I was hoping that she'd leave and Albright would come and I'd be back in my house before midnight.

"It's pretty out here, huh?" Her voice came from behind me.

"Yeah. It's all right."

"I come from Des Moines, in Iowa. They don't have anything like the ocean back there. Are you from L.A.?"

"No. Texas." The back of my scalp was tingling.

"Do they have an ocean in Texas?"

"The Gulf, they have the Gulf."

"So you're used to it." She leaned on the rail next to me. "It still knocks me out whenever I see it. My name's Barbara. Barbara Moskowitz. That's a Jewish name."

"Ezekiel Rawlins," I whispered. I didn't want her so familiar as to use my nickname. When I glanced over my shoulder I noticed that a couple of the young men were looking around, like they'd lost someone.

"I think they're looking for you," I said.

"Who cares?" she answered. "My sister just brought me 'cause my parents made her. All she wants to do is make out with Herman and smoke cigarettes."

"It's still dangerous for a girl to be alone. Your parents are right to want you with somebody."

"Are you going to hurt me?" She stared into my face intently. I remember wondering what color her eyes were before I heard the shouting.

"Hey you! Black boy! What's happening here?" It was a pimply-faced boy. He couldn't have been more than twenty years and five and a half feet but he came up to me like a full-grown soldier. He wasn't afraid; a regular fool of a youth.

"What do you want?" I asked as politely as I could.

"You know what I mean," he said as he came within range of my grasp.

"Leave him alone, Herman!" Barbara yelled. "We were just talking!"

"You were, huh?" he said to me. "We don't need ya talking to our women."

I could have broken his neck. I could have put out his eyes or broken all of his fingers. But instead I held my breath.

Five of his friends were headed toward us. While they were coming on, not yet organized or together, I could have killed all of them too. What did they know about violence? I could have crushed their windpipes one by one and they couldn't have done a thing to stop me. They couldn't even run fast enough to escape me. I was still a killing machine.

"Hey!" the tallest one said. "What's wrong?"

"Nigger's trying to pick up Barbara."

"Yeah, an' she's just jailbait."

"Leave him alone!" Barbara shouted. "He was just saying where he was from."

I guess she was trying to help me, like a mother hugging her child when he's just broken his ribs.

"Barbara!" another girl shouted.

"Hey, man, what's wrong with you?" the big one asked in my face. He was wide-shouldered and a little taller than I; built like a football player. He had a broad, fleshy face. His eyes, nose, and mouth were like tiny islands on a great sea of white skin.

I noticed that a couple of the others had picked up sticks. They moved in around me, forcing me back against the rail.

"I don't want any problem, man," I said. I could smell the liquor on the tall one's breath.

"You already got a problem, boy."

"Listen, all she said was hi. That's all I said too." But I was thinking to myself, Why the hell do I have to answer to you?

Herman said, "He was tellin' her where he lived. She said so herself."

I was trying to remember how far down the beach was. By then I knew I had to get out of there before there were two or three dead bodies, one of them being mine.

"Excuse me," a man's voice called out.

There was a slight commotion behind the football player and then a Panama hat appeared there next to him.

"Excuse me," Mr. DeWitt Albright said again. He was smiling.

"What do you want?" the footballer said.

DeWitt just smiled and then he pulled the pistol, which looked somewhat like a rifle, from his coat. He leveled the barrel at the large boy's right eye and said, "I want to see your brains scattered all over your friends' clothes, son. I want you to die for me."

The large boy, who was wearing red swimming trunks, made a sound like he had swallowed his tongue. He moved his shoulder ever so slightly and DeWitt cocked back the hammer. It sounded like a bone breaking.

"I wouldn't move if I were you, son. I mean, if you were to breathe too heavily I'd just kill you. And if any of you other boys move I'll kill him and then I'll shoot off *all* your nuts."

The ocean was rumbling and the air had turned cold. The only human sound was from Barbara, who was sobbing in her sister's arms.

"I want you boys to meet my friend," DeWitt said. "Mr. Jones."

I didn't know what to do so I nodded.

"He's a friend'a mine," Mr. Albright continued. "And I'd be proud and happy if he was to lower himself to fuck my sister *and* my mother."

No one had anything to say to that.

"Now, Mr. Jones, I want to ask you something."

"Yes, sir, Mr., ah, Smith."

"Do you think that I should shoot out this nasty's boy's eye-ball?"

I let that question hang for a bit. Two of the younger boys had been weeping already but the wait caused the footballer to start crying.

"Well," I said, after fifteen seconds or so, "if he's not sorry for bullying me then I think you should kill him."

"I'm sorry," said the boy.

"You are?" Mr. Albright asked.

"Y-y-yes!"

"How sorry are you? I mean, are you sorry enough?"

"Yessir, I am."

"You're sorry enough?" When he asked that question he moved the muzzle of the gun close enough to touch the boy's tiny, flickering eyelid. "Don't twitch now, I want you to see the bullet coming. Now are you sorry enough?"

"Yessir!"

"Then prove it. I want you to show him. I want you to get down on your knees and suck his peter. I want you to suck it good now . . ."

The boy started crying outright when Albright said that. I was pretty confident that he was just joking, in a sick kind of way, but my heart quailed along with the footballer.

"Down on your knees or you're dead, boy!"

The other boys had their eyes glued to the footballer as he went to his knees. They tore out running when Albright slammed the barrel of his pistol into the side of the boy's head.

"Get out of here!" Albright yelled. "And if you tell some cops I'll find every one of you."

We were alone in less than half a minute. I could hear the slamming of car doors and the revving of jalopy engines from the parking lot and the street.

"They got something to think about now," Albright said. He returned his long-barreled .44-caliber pistol to the holster inside his coat. The pier was abandoned; everything was dark and silent.

"I don't think that they'd dare call the cops on something like this but we should move on just in case," he said.


Albright's white Cadillac was parked in the lot down under the pier. He drove south down along the ocean. There were few electric lights from the coast, and just a sliver of moon, but the sea glittered with a million tiny glints. It looked like every shiny fish in the sea had come to the surface to mimic the stars that flickered in the sky. There was light everywhere and there was darkness everywhere too.

He switched on the radio and tuned in a big-band station that was playing "Two Lonely People," by Fats Waller. I remember because as soon as the music came on I started shivering. I wasn't afraid; I was angry, angry at the way he humiliated that boy. I didn't care about the boy's feelings, I cared that if Albright could do something like that to one of his own then I knew he could do the same, and much worse, to me. But if he wanted to shoot me he'd just have to do it because I wasn't going down on my knees for him or for anybody else.

I never doubted for a minute that Albright would have killed that boy.

"What you got, Easy?" he asked after a while.

"I got a name and an address. I got the last day she was seen and who she was with. I know the man she was seen with and I know what he does for a living." I was proud of knowledge when I was a young man. Joppy had told me just to take the money and to pretend I was looking for the girl, but once I had a piece of information I had to show it off.

"All that's worth the money."

"But I want to know something first."

"What's that?" Mr. Albright asked. He pulled the car onto a shoulder that overlooked the shimmering Pacific. The waves were really rolling that night, you could even hear them through the closed windows.

"I want to know that no harm is going to come to that girl, or anybody else."

"Do I look that much like God to you? Can I tell you what will happen tomorrow? I don't plan for the girl to be hurt. My friend thinks he's in love with her. He wants to buy her a gold ring and live happily ever after. But, you know, she might forget to buckle her shoes next week and fall down and break her neck, and if she does you can't hold me up for it. But whatever."

I knew that was the most I would get out of him. DeWitt made no promises but I believed that he meant no harm to the girl in the photograph.

"She was with a man named Frank Green, Tuesday last. They were at a bar called the Playroom."

"Where is she now?"

"Woman who told me said she thought that they were a team, Green and the girl, so she's probably with him."

"Where's that?" he asked. His smile and good manners were gone; this was business now—plain and simple.

"He's got an apartment at Skyler and Eighty-third. Place is called the Skyler Arms."

He took out the white pen and wallet and scribbled something on the notepad. Then he stared at me with those dead eyes while he tapped the steering wheel with the pen.

"What else?"

"Frank's a gangster," I said. That got DeWitt to smile again. "He's with hijackers. They take liquor and cigarettes; sell'em all over southern California."

"Bad man?" DeWitt couldn't keep his smile down.

"Bad enough. He somethin' with a knife."

"You ever see him in action? I mean, you see him kill somebody?"

"I saw him cut a man in a bar once; loudmouth dude didn't know who Frank was."

DeWitt's eyes came to life for a moment; he leaned across the seat so far that I could feel his dry breath on my neck. "I want you to remember something, Easy. I want you to think about when Frank took his knife and stabbed that man."

I thought about it a second and then I nodded to let him know that I was ready.

"Before he went at him, did he hesitate? Even for a second?"

I thought about the crowded bar down on Figueroa. The big man was talking to Frank's woman and when Frank walked up to him he put his hand against Frank's chest, getting ready to push him away, I suppose. Frank's eyes widened and he threw his head around as if to say to the crowd, "Look at what this fool is doin'! He deserve t'be dead, stupid as he acts!" Then the knife appeared in Frank's hand and the big man crumpled against the bar, trying to ward off the stroke with his big fleshy arms . . .

"Maybe just a second, not even that," I said.

Mr. DeWitt Albright laughed softly.

"Well," he said. "I guess I have to see what I shall see."

"Maybe you could get to the girl when he's out. Frank spends a lot of time on the road. I saw him the other night, at John's, he

was dressed for hijacking, so he might be out of town for a couple
of more days."

"That would be best," Albright answered. He leaned back
across the seat. "No reason to be any messier than we have to,
now. You got that photograph?"

"No," I lied. "Not on me. I left it at home."

He only looked at me for a second but I knew he didn't believe
it. I don't know why I wanted to keep her picture. It's just that the
way she looked out at me made me feel good.

"Well, maybe I'll pick it up after I find her; you know I like to
make everything neat after a job . . . Here's another hundred and
take this card too. All you have to do is go down to that address
and you can pick up a job to tide you over until something else
comes up."

He handed me a tight roll of bills and a card. I couldn't read the
card in that dim light so I shoved it and the money in my pocket.

"I think I can get my old job back so I won't need the address."

"Hold on to it," he said, as he turned the ignition. "You did
alright by me, getting this information, and I'm doing right by
you. That's the way I do business, Easy; I always pay my debts."


The drive back was quiet and brilliant with night lights. Benny
Goodman was on the radio and DeWitt Albright hummed along
as if he had grown up with big bands.

When we pulled up to my car, next to the pier, everything was
as it had been when we left. When I opened the door to get out
Albright said, "Pleasure working with you, Easy." He extended
his hand and when he had the snake grip on me again his look
became quizzical and he said, "You know, I was wondering just
one thing."

"What's that?"

"How come you let those boys get around you like that? You

could have picked them off one by one before they got your back to the rails."

"I don't kill children," I said.

Albright laughed for the second time that night.

Then he let me go and said goodbye.

**O**ur team worked in a large hangar on the south side of the Santa Monica plant. I got there early, about 6 A.M., before the day shift began. I wanted to get to Benny, Benito Giacomo, before they started working.

Once Champion designed a new aircraft, either for the air force or for one of the airlines, they had a few teams build them for a while to get out the kinks in construction. Benito's team would, for instance, put together the left wing and move it on to another group in charge of assembly for the entire aircraft. But instead of assembling the plane a group of experts would go over our work with a magnifying glass to make sure that the procedures they set up for production were good.

It was an important job and all the men were proud to be on it but Benito was so high-strung that whenever we had a new project he'd turn sour.

That's really why he fired me.

I was coming off of a hard shift, we had two men out with the flu, and I was tired. Benny wanted us to stay longer just to check out our work but I didn't want any of it. I was tired and I knew that anything I looked at would have gotten a passing grade, so I said that we should wait until morning. The men listened to me. I wasn't a team leader but Benny relied on me to set an example for others because I was such a good worker. But that was just a bad day. I needed sleep to do the job right and Benny didn't trust me enough to hear that.

He told me that I had to work hard if I wanted to get the promotion we'd talked about; a promotion that would put me just a grade below Dupree.

I told him that I worked hard every day.

A job in a factory is an awful lot like working on a plantation·in the South. The bosses see all the workers like they're children, and everyone knows how lazy children are. So Benny thought he'd teach me a little something about responsibility because he was the boss and I was the child.

The white workers didn't have a problem with that kind of treatment because they didn't come from a place where men were always called boys. The white worker would have just said, "Sure, Benny, you called it right, but damn if I can see straight right now." And Benny would have understood that. He would have laughed and realized how pushy he was being and offered to take Mr. Davenport, or whoever, out to drink a beer. But the Negro workers didn't drink with Benny. We didn't go to the same bars, we didn't wink at the same girls.

What I should have done, if I wanted my job, was to stay, like he asked, and then come back early the next day to recheck the work.

If I had told Benny I couldn't see straight he would have told me to buy glasses.


So there I was at the mouth of the man-made cave of an airplane hangar. The sun wasn't really up but everything was light. The large cement floor was empty except for a couple of trucks and a large tarp over the wing assembly. It felt good and familiar to be back there. No jazzy photographs of white girls anywhere, no strange white men with dead blue eyes. I was in a place of family men and working men who went home to their own houses at night and read the newspaper and watched Milton Berle.

"Easy!"

Dupree's shout always sounded the same whether he was happy to see you or he was about to pull out his small-barreled pistol.

"Hey, Dupree!" I shouted.

"What you say to Coretta, man?" he asked as he came up to me.

"Nuthin', nuthin' at all. What you mean?"

"Well, either you said sumpin' or I got bad breath because she tore out yesterday mornin' an' I ain't seen'er since."

"What?"

"Yeah! She fixed me some breakfast an' then said she had some business so she'd see me fo' dinner and that's the last I seen of'er."

"She din't come home?"

"Nope. You know I come in an' burnt some pork chops to make up for the night before but she din't come in."

Dupree had a couple of inches on me and he was built like Joppy when Joppy was still a boxer. He was hovering over me and I could feel the violence come off of him in waves.

"No, man, I didn't say a thing. We put you in the bed, then she gave me a drink and I went home. That's all."

"Then where is she?" he demanded.

"How you expect me t'know? You know Coretta. She likes to keep her secrets. Maybe she's with her auntie out in Compton. She could be in Reno."

Dupree relaxed a little and laughed. "You prob'ly right, Easy. Coretta hear them slot machines goin' an' she leave her own momma."

He slapped me on the back and laughed again.

I swore to myself that I'd never look at another man's woman. I've taken that pledge many times since then.

"Rawlins," came a voice from the small office at the back of the hangar.

"There you go," Dupree said.

I walked toward the man who had called me. The office he stood before was a prefabricated green shell, more like a tent than a room. Benny kept his desk in there and only went in himself to meet with the bosses or to fire one of the men. He called me in there four days before to tell me that Champion couldn't use men that didn't give "a little extra."

"Mr. Giacomo," I said. We shook but there was no friendliness in it.

Benny was shorter than I but he had broad shoulders and big hands. His salt-and-pepper hair had once been jet black and his skin color was darker than many mulattos I'd known. But Benny was a white man and I was a Negro. He wanted me to work hard for him and he needed me to be grateful that he allowed me to work at all. His eyes were close-set so he looked intent. His shoulders were slightly hunched, which made him seem like an advancing boxer.

"Easy," he said.

We went into the shell and he pointed at a chair. He took a seat behind the desk, kicked his foot up on it, and lit a cigarette.

"Dupree says that you want back on the job, Easy."

I was thinking that Benny probably had a bottle of rye in the bottom drawer of his desk.

"Sure, Mr. Giacomo, you know I need this job to eat." I concentrated on keeping my head erect. I wasn't going to bow down to him.

"Well, you know that when you fire somebody you have to stick to your guns. The men might get to thinkin' that I'm weak if I take you back."

"So what am I doin' here?" I said to his face.

He leaned farther back in his chair and hunched his large shoulders. "You tell me."

"Dupree said that you would give me my job back."

"I don't know who gave him the authority to say that. All I said was that I'd be glad to talk to you if you had something to say. Do you have something to say?"

I tried to think about what Benny wanted. I tried to think of how I could save face and still kiss his ass. But all I could really think about was that other office and that other white man. De-Witt Albright had his bottle and his gun right out there in plain view. When he asked me what I had to say I told him; I might have been a little nervous, but I told him anyway. Benny didn't care about what I had to say. He needed all his children to kneel down and let him be the boss. He wasn't a businessman, he was a plantation boss; a slaver.

"Well, Easy?"

"I want my job back, Mr. Giacomo. I need to work and I do a good job."

"Is that all?"

"No, that's not all. I need money so that I can pay my mortgage and eat. I need a house to live in and a place to raise children. I need to buy clothes so I can go to the pool hall and to church . . ."

Benny put his feet down and made to rise. "I have to get back to my job, Easy . . ."

"That's Mr. Rawlins!" I said as I rose to meet him. "You don't have to give me my job back but you have got to treat me with respect."

"Excuse me," he said. He made to go past me but I was blocking his way.

"I said, you have got to treat me with respect. Now I call you Mr. Giacomo because that's your name. You're no friend to me and I got no reason to be disrespectful and call you by your first name." I pointed at my chest. "My name is Mr. Rawlins."

He balled his fists and looked down at my chest the way a fighter does. But I think he heard the quaver in my voice. He knew that one or two of us would be broken up if he tried to go through me. And who knows? Maybe he realized that he was in the wrong.

"I'm sorry, Mr. Rawlins," he smiled at me. "But there are no openings right now. Maybe you could come back in a few months, when production on the new fighter line begins."

With that he motioned for me to leave his office. I went without another word.

I looked around for Dupree but he was nowhere to be seen, not even at his station. That surprised me but I was too happy to worry about him. My chest was heaving and I felt as if I wanted to laugh out loud. My bills were paid and it felt good to have stood up for myself. I had a notion of freedom when I walked out to my car.

I was home by noon. The street was empty and the neighborhood was quiet. There was a dark Ford parked across the street from my house. I remember thinking that a bill collector was making his rounds. Then I laughed to myself because all my bills were paid well in advance. I was a proud man that day; my fall wasn't far behind.

As I was closing the gate to the front yard I saw the two white men getting out of the Ford. One was tall and skinny and he was wearing a dark blue suit. The other one was my height and three times my girth. He had on a wrinkled tan suit that had greasy spots here and there.

The men strode quickly in my direction but I just turned slowly and walked toward my door.

"Mr. Rawlins!" one of them called from behind.

I turned. "Yeah?"

They were approaching fast but cautiously. The fat one had a hand in his pocket.

"Mr. Rawlins, I'm Miller and this is my partner Mason." They both held out badges.

"Yeah?"

"We want you to come with us."

"Where?"

"You'll see," fat Mason said as he took me by the arm.

"Are you arresting me?"

"You'll see," Mason said again. He was pulling me toward the gate.

"I've got the right to know why you're taking me."

"You got a right to fall down and break your face, nigger. You got a right to die," he said. Then he hit me in the diaphragm. When I doubled over he slipped the handcuffs on behind my back and together they dragged me to the car. They tossed me in the back seat where I lay gagging.

"You vomit on my carpet and I'll feed it to ya," Mason called back.

They drove me to the Seventy-seventh Street station and carried me in the front door.

"You got'im, huh, Miller?" somebody said. They were holding me by my arms and I was sagging with my head down. I had recovered from the punch but I didn't want them to know it.

"Yeah, we got him coming home. Nothing on'im."

They opened the door to a small room that smelled faintly of urine. The walls were unpainted plaster and there was only a bare wooden chair for furniture. They didn't offer me the chair though, they just dropped me on my knees and walked out, closing the door behind them.

The door had a tiny peephole in it.

I pushed my shoulder against the wall until I was standing. The room didn't look any better. There were a few bare pipes along the ceiling that dripped now and then. The edge of the linoleum floor was corroded and chalky from the moisture. There was only one window. It didn't have glass but only a crisscross of two two-inch bars down and two bars across. Very little light came in through the window due to the branches and leaves that had pushed their way in. It was a small room, maybe twelve by twenty, and I had some fear that it was to be the last room I ever inhabited.

I was worried because they didn't follow the routine. I had played the game of "cops and nigger" before. The cops pick you up, take your name and fingerprints, then they throw you into a holding tank with other "suspects" and drunks. After you were sick from the vomit and foul language they'd take you to another room and ask why you robbed that liquor store or what did you do with the money?

I would try to look innocent while I denied what they said. It's hard acting innocent when you are but the cops know that you aren't. They figure that you did something because that's just the way cops think, and you telling them that you're innocent just proves to them that you have something to hide. But that wasn't the game that we were playing that day. They knew my name and they didn't need to scare me with any holding tank; they didn't need to take my fingerprints. I didn't know why they had me, but I did know that it didn't matter as long as they thought they were right.

I sat down in the chair and looked up at the leaves coming in through the window. I counted thirty-two bright green oleander leaves. Also coming in through the window was a line of black ants that ran down the side of the wall and around to the other side of the room where the tiny corpse of a mouse was crushed into a corner. I speculated that another prisoner had killed the mouse by stamping it. He probably had tried in the middle of the floor at first but the quick rodent had swerved away two, maybe even three times. But finally the mouse made the deadly mistake of looking for a crevice in the wall and the inmate was able to block off his escape by using both feet. The mouse looked papery and dry so I supposed that the death had occurred at the beginning of the week; about the time I was getting fired.

While I was thinking about the mouse the door opened again and the officers stepped in. I was angry at myself because I hadn't tried to see if the door was locked. Those cops had me where they wanted me.

"Ezekiel Rawlins," Miller said.

"Yes, sir."

"We have a few questions to ask. We can take off those cuffs if you want to start cooperating."

"I am cooperating."

"Told ya, Bill," fat Mason said. "He's a smart nigger."

"Take off the cuffs, Charlie," Miller said and the fat man obliged.

"Where were you yesterday morning at about 5 A.M.?"

"What morning is that?" I stalled.

"He means," fat Mason said as he planted his foot in my chest and pushed me over backwards, "Thursday morning."

"Get up," Miller said.

I got to my feet and righted the chair.

"That's hard to say." I sat down again. "I was out drinking and then I helped carry a drunk friend home. I could'a been on my way home or maybe I was already in bed. I didn't look at a clock."

"What friend is that?"

"Pete. My friend Pete."

"Pete, huh?" Mason chuckled. He wandered over to my left and before I could turn toward him I felt the hard knot of his fist explode against the side of my head.

I was on the ground again.

"Get up," Miller said.

I got up again.

"So where was you and your peter drinkin'?" Mason sneered.

"Down at a friend's on Eighty-nine."

Mason moved again but this time I turned. He just looked at me with an innocent face and his palms turned upward.

"Would that be an illegal nightclub called John's?" Miller asked.

I was quiet.

"You got bigger problems than busting your friend's bar, Ezekiel. You got bigger troubles than that."

"What kinds troubles?"

"Big troubles."

"What's that mean?"

"Means we can take your black ass out behind the station and put a bullet in your head," Mason said.

"Where were you at five o'clock on Thursday morning, Mr. Rawlins?" Miller asked.

"I don't know exactly."

Mason had taken off his shoe and started swatting the heel against his fat palm.

"Five o'clock," Miller said.

We played that game a little while longer. Finally I said, "Look, you don't have to beat up your hand on my account; I'm happy to tell you what you wanna know."

"You ready to cooperate?" Miller asked.

"Yes, sir."

"Where did you go when you left Coretta James' house on Thursday morning?"

"I went home."

Mason tried to kick the chair out from under me but I was on my feet before he could.

"I had enough'a this shit, man!" I yelled, but neither cop seemed very impressed. "I told you I went home, and that's all."

"Have a seat, Mr. Rawlins," Miller said calmly.

"Why'm I gonna sit and you keep tryin' to knock me down?" I cried. But I sat down anyway.

"I told ya he was crazy, Bill," Mason said. "I told ya this was a section eight."

"Mr. Rawlins," Miller said. "Where did you go after you left Miss James' house?"

"I went home."

No one hit me that time; no one tried to kick the chair.

"Did you see Miss James later that day?"

"No, sir."

"Did you have an altercation with Mr. Bouchard?"

I understood him but I said, "Huh?"

"Did you and Dupree Bouchard have words over Miss James?"

"You know," Mason chimed in. "Pete."

"That's what I call him sometimes," I said.

"Did you," Miller repeated, "have an altercation with Mr. Bouchard?"

"I didn't have nuthin' with Dupree. He was asleep."

"So where did you go on Thursday?"

"I went home with a hangover. I stayed there all day and night and then I went to work today. Well"—I wanted to keep them talking so that Mason wouldn't lose his temper with the furniture again—"not to work really because I got fired Monday. But I went to get my job back."

"Where did you go on Thursday?"

"I went home with a hangover . . ."

"Nigger!" Mason tore into me with his fists. He knocked me to the floor but I grabbed onto his wrists. I swung around and twisted so that I was straddling his back, sitting on his fat ass. I could have killed him the way I'd killed other white men in uniforms, but I could feel Miller behind me so I stood straight up and moved to the corner.

Miller had a police special in his hand.

Mason made like he was going to come after me again but the belly-flop had winded him. From his knees Mason said, "Lemme have'im alone fer a minute."

Miller weighed the request. He kept looking back and forth between me and the fat man. Maybe he was afraid that I'd kill his partner or maybe he didn't want the paperwork; it could have been that Miller was a secret humanitarian who didn't want bloodshed and ruin on his hands. Finally he whispered, "No."

"But . . . ," Mason started.

"I said no. Let's move."

Miller hooked his free hand under the fat man's armpit and helped him to his feet. Then he holstered his pistol and straightened his coat. Mason sneered at me and then followed Miller out of the cell door. He was starting to remind me of a trained mutt. The lock snapped behind them.

I got back in the chair and counted the leaves again. I followed the ants to the dead mouse again. This time though, I imagined that I was the convict and that mouse was officer Mason. I crushed him so that his whole suit was soiled and shapeless in the corner; his eyes came out of his head.

There was a light bulb hanging from a wire at the ceiling but there was no way to turn it on. Slowly the little sun that filtered in through the leaves faded and the room became twilight. I sat in the chair pressing my bruises now and then to see if the pain was lessening.

I didn't think a thing. I didn't wonder about Coretta or Dupree or how the police knew so much about my Wednesday night. All I did was sit in darkness, trying to become the darkness. I was awake but my thinking was like a dream. I dreamed in my wakefulness that I could become the darkness and slip out between the eroded cracks of that cell. If I was nighttime nobody could find me; no one would even know I was missing.

I saw faces in the darkness; beautiful women and feasts of ham and pie. It's only now that I realize how lonely and hungry I was then.

It was fully black in that cell when the light snapped on. I was still trying to blink away the glare when Miller and Mason came in. Miller closed the door.

"You think of anything else to say?" Miller asked me.

I just looked at him.

"You can go," Miller said.

"You heard him, nigger!" Mason shouted while he was fumbling around to check that his fly was zipped up. "Get outta here!"

They led me into the open room and past the desk watch. Everywhere people turned to stare at me. Some laughed, some were shocked.

They took me to the desk sergeant, who handed me my wallet and pocketknife.

"We might be in touch with you later, Mr. Rawlins," Miller said. "If we have any questions we know where you live."

"Questions about what?" I asked, trying to sound like an honest man asking an honest question.

"That's police business."

"Ain't it my business if you drag me outta my own yard an' bring me down here an' throw me around?"

"You want a complaint form?" Miller's thin, gray face didn't change expression. He looked like a man I once knew, Orrin Clay. Orrin had a peptic ulcer and always held his mouth like he was just about to spit.

"I wanna know what's goin' on," I said.

"We'll be coming 'round if we need you."

"How am I supposed to get home from way out here? The buses stop after six."

Miller turned away from me. Mason was already gone.

left the station at a fast walk but I wanted to run.

It was fifteen blocks to John's speak and I had to keep telling myself to slow down. I knew that a patrol car would arrest any sprinting Negro they encountered.

The streets were especially dark and empty. Central Avenue was like a giant black alley and I felt like a small rat, hugging the corners and looking out for cats.

Every once in a while a car would shoot past. Maybe I'd catch a snatch of music or laughter and then they'd be gone. There wasn't another soul out walking.

I was three blocks from the station when I heard, "Hey you! Easy Rawlins!"

A black Cadillac had pulled up beside me and matched my pace. It was a long automobile; long enough to be two cars. A white face in a black cap stuck out of the driver's window. "Come on, Easy, over here," the face said.

"Who are you?" I asked over my shoulder, then I turned to keep on walking.

"Come on, Easy," the face said again. "Somebody in the back wants to talk to you."

"I don't have the time right now, man. I gotta go." I had doubled my pace so that I was nearly running.

"Jump in. We'll take you where you're going," he said, and then he said "What?" not to me but to whoever his passenger was.

"Easy," he said again. I hate it when someone I don't know knows my by name. "My boss wants to give you fifty dollars to take a ride."

"Ride where?" I didn't slow my stride.

"Wherever you want to go."

I stopped talking and kept on walking.

The Cadillac sped on ahead and pulled onto the curb about thirty feet ahead of me. The driver's door swung open and he came out. He had to unfold his long legs from his chest to climb out from the seat. When he stood up I could see that he was a tall man with a thin, almost crescent face and light hair that was either gray or blond—I couldn't tell which by lamplight.

He held his hands out in front of him, about shoulder height. It was a strange gesture because it looked like he was asking for peace but I knew he could have grabbed me from that pose too.

"Listen here, man," I said. I crouched back thinking that it would be easiest to take a tall man down at the knee. "I'm goin' home. That's all I'm doin'. Your friend wanna talk, then you better tell'im to get me on the phone."

The tall driver pointed behind with his thumb and said, "Man told me to tell you that he knows why the police took you in, Easy. He says he wants to talk about it."

The driver had a grin on his face and faraway look in his eye.

While I looked at him I got tired. I felt that if I lunged at him I'd just fall on my face. Anyway, I wanted to find out why the police had taken me in.

"Just talk, right?" I asked.

"If he wanted to hurt you you'd already be dead."

The driver opened the door to the back seat and I climbed in. The moment the door shut I gagged on the odors. The smells were sweet like perfume and sour, an odor of the body that I recognized but could put no name to.

The car took off in reverse and I was thrown into the seat with my back to the driver. Before me sat a fat white man. His round white face looked like a moon in the flashes of passing lamplight. He was smiling. Behind his seat was a shallow storage area. I thought I saw something moving around back there but before I could look closer he spoke to me.

"Where is she, Mr. Rawlins?"

" 'Scuse me?"

"Daphne Monet. Where is she?"

"Who's that?"

I never got used to big lips on white people, especially white men. This white man had lips that were fat and red. They looked like swollen wounds.

"I know why they took you in there, Mr. Rawlins." He gestured with his head to say the police station behind. But when he did that I looked in the storage area again. He looked pleased and said, "Come on out, honey."

A small boy climbed over the seat. He was wearing soiled briefs and dirty white socks. His skin was brown and his thick straight hair was black. The almond-shaped eyes spoke of China but this was a Mexican boy.

He climbed down to the floor and curled around the fat man's leg.

"This is my little man," the fat man said. "He's the only reason I can keep on going."

The sight of that poor child and the odors made me cringe. I tried not to think about what I was seeing because I couldn't do anything about it—at least not right then.

"I don't know what you want with me, Mr. Teran," I said. "But I don't know why the police arrested me and I don't know no Daphne nobody. All I want is to get home and put this whole night behind me."

"So you know who I am?"

"I read the paper. You were running for mayor."

"Could be again," he said. "Could be again. And maybe you could help." He reached down to scratch the little boy behind the ear.

"I don't know what you mean. I don't know nuthin'."

"The police wanted to know what you did after you had drinks with Coretta James and Dupree Bouchard."

"Yeah?"

"I don't care about that, Easy. All I want to know is if somebody used the name Daphne Monet."

I shook my head, no.

"Did anybody," he hesitated, "strange . . . want to talk to Coretta?"

"What you mean, strange?"

Matthew Teran smiled at me for a moment, then he said, "Daphne is a white girl, Easy. Young and pretty. It means an awful lot to me if I can find her."

"I can't help ya, man. I don't even know why they pulled me in there. Do you know?"

Instead of answering me he asked, "Did you know Howard Green?"

"I met'im once or twice."

"Did Coretta say anything about him that night?"

"Not a word." It felt good to tell the truth.

"How about your friend Dupree? Did he say anything?"

"Dupree drinks. That's what he does. And when he's finished

drinking, then he goes to sleep. That's what he did. That's all he did."

"I'm a powerful man, Mr. Rawlins." He didn't need to tell me. "And I wouldn't want to think that you were lying to me."

"Do you know why the cops took me in?"

Matthew Teran picked up the little Mexican boy and hugged him to his chest.

"What do you think, honey?" he asked the boy.

Thick mucus threatened to flow from the boy's nose. His mouth was open and he stared at me as if I were a strange animal. Not a dangerous animal, maybe the corpse of a dog or porcupine run over and bleeding on the highway.

Mr. Teran picked up an ivory horn that hung next to his head and spoke into it. "Norman, take Mr. Rawlins where he wants to go. We're finished for the time being." Then he handed the horn to me. It smelled strongly of sweet oils and sour bodies. I tried to ignore the smells as I gave Norman the address of John's speak.

"Here's your money, Mr. Rawlins," Teran said. He was holding a few damp bills in his hand.

"No thanks." I didn't want to touch anything that that man had touched.

"My office is listed in the book, Mr. Rawlins. If you find something out I think you might find me helpful."

When the car stopped in front of John's I got out as fast as I could.

"Easy!" Hattie yelled. "What happened to you, baby?"

She came around the counter to put her hand on my shoulder.

"Cops," I said.

"Oh, baby. Was it about Coretta?"

Everyone seemed to know about my life.

"What about Coretta?"

"Ain't you heard?"

I just stared at her.

"Coretta been murdered," she said. "I hear the police took Dupree outta his job 'cause he been out there with her. And I knowed you was with'em on Wednesday so I figured the police might'a s'pected you."

"Murdered?"

"Just like Howard Green. Beat her so bad that it was her mother who had to tell'em."

"Dead?"

"What they do to you, Easy?"

"Is Odell here, Hattie?"

"Come in 'bout seven."

"What time is it?"

"Ten."

"Could you get Odell for me?" I asked.

"Sure can, Easy. You just let me get Junior t'do it."

She stuck her head in the door and then came back. In a few minutes Odell came out. I could see that I must've looked bad by the expression on Odell's face. He rarely showed any emotion at all but right then he looked like he'd seen a ghost.

"Could you give me a ride home, Odell? I don't have my car."

"Sure thing, Easy."


Odell was quiet for most of the ride but when we got close to my house he said, "You better get some rest, Easy."

"I sure intend to try, Odell."

"I don't mean just sleep, now. I mean some real rest, like a vacation or somethin'."

I laughed. "A woman once told me that poor people can't afford no vacations. She said that we gotta keep workin' or we end up dead."

"You don't have to stop workin'. I mean more like a change.

Maybe you should go on down t'Houston or maybe even Galveston where they don't know you too good."

"Why you say that, Odell?"

We pulled up to my house. My Pontiac was a welcome sight, parked there and waiting for me. I could have driven across the nation with the money Albright had given me.

"First Howard Green gets killed, then Coretta goes the same way. Police do this to you and they say Dupree's still in jail. Time to go."

"I can't go, Odell."

"Why not?"

I looked at my house. My beautiful home.

"I just can't," I said. "But I do think you're right."

"If you don't leave, Easy, then you better look for some help."

"What kind'a help you mean?"

"I don't know. Maybe you should come on down to church on Sunday. Maybe you could talk to Reverend Towne."

"Lord ain't got no succor fo' this mess. I'm'a have to look somewhere else."

I got out of his car and waved him goodbye. But Odell was a good friend; he waited there until I had hobbled to my door and stumbled into the house.

I put away a pint and a half of bourbon before I could get to sleep. The sheets were crisp and dry and the fear was far enough away in the alcohol, but whenever I closed my eyes Coretta was there, hunching over me and kissing my chest.

I was still young enough that I couldn't imagine death really happening to someone I knew. Even in the war I expected to see friends again, though I knew they were dead.

The night carried on like that. I'd fall asleep for a few minutes only to wake up calling Coretta's name or to answer her calling me. If I couldn't fall back to sleep I'd reach for the bottle of whiskey next to the bed.


Later that night the phone rang.

"Huh?" I mumbled.

"Easy? Easy, that you?" came a rough voice.

"Yeah. What time is it?"

" 'Bout three. You 'sleep, man?"

"What you think? Who is this?"

"Junior. Don't you know me?"

It took me a while to remember who he was. Junior and I had never been friends and I couldn't even think of where he might have found my phone number.

"Easy? Easy! You fallin' back asleep?"

"What you want this time'a mornin', Junior?"

"Ain't nuthin'. Nuthin'."

"Nuthin'? You gonna get me outta my bed at three fo' nuthin'?"

"Don't go soundin' off on me now, man. I just wanted to tell you what you wanted t'know."

"What you want, Junior?"

" 'Bout that girl, thas all." He sounded nervous. He was talking fast and I had the feeling that he kept looking over his shoulder. "Why was you lookin' fo' her anyway?"

"You mean the white girl?"

"Yeah. I just remembered that I saw her last week. She come in with Frank Green."

"What's her name?"

"I think he called her Daphne. I think."

"So how come you just tellin' me now? How come you callin' me this late anyway?"

"I'ont get off till two-thirty, Easy. I thought you wanted to know, so I called ya."

"You jus' figgered you'd call me in the middle'a the night an' tell me 'bout some girl? Man, you fulla shit! What the hell do you want?"

Junior let out a couple of curses and hung the phone in my ear.

I got the bottle and poured myself a tall drink. Then I lit up a cigarette and pondered Junior's call. It didn't make any sense, him calling me in the night just to tell me about some girl I wanted to play with. He had to know something. But what could a thick-headed field hand like Junior know about my business? I finished the drink and the cigarette but it still didn't make sense.

The whiskey calmed my nerves, though, and I was able to fall into a half sleep. I dreamed about casting for catfish down south of Houston when I was just a boy. There were giant catfish in the Gatlin River. My mother told me that some of them were so big that the alligators left them alone.

I had caught on to one of those giants and I could just make out its big head below the surface of the water. Its snout was the size of a man's torso.

Then the phone rang.

I couldn't answer it without losing my fish so I shouted for my mother to get it but she must not have heard because the phone kept on ringing and that catfish kept trying to dive. I finally had to let it go and I was almost crying when I picked up the receiver. "Hello."

" 'Allo? Thees is Mr. Rawlins? Yes?" The accent was mild, like French, but it wasn't French exactly.

"Yeah," I exhaled. "Who's that?"

"I am calling you about a problem with a friend of yours."

"Who's that?"

"Coretta James," she said, enunciating each syllable.

That set me up straight. "Who is this?"

"My name is Daphne. Daphne Monet," she said. "Your friend, Coretta, no? She came to see me and asked for money. She said that you were looking for me and if I don't give it to her she goes to tell you. Easy, no?"

"When she say that?"

"Not yesterday but the day before that."

"So what'd you do?"

"I give to her my last twenty dollars. I don't know you, do I, Mr. Rawlins?"

"What she do then?"

"She goes away and I worry about it and my friend is away and doesn't come back home so then I think maybe I find you and you tell me, yes? Why you want to find me?"

"I don't know what you mean," I said. "But your friend, who's that?"

"Frank. Frank Green."

I reached for my pants out of reflex; they were on the floor, next to the bed.

"Why do you look for me, Mr. Rawlins? Do I know you?"

"You must'a made some kinda mistake, honey. I don't know what she was talkin' 'bout . . . Do you think Frank went lookin' for her?"

"I don't tell Frank about her coming 'ere. He was not 'ere but then he does not come home."

"I don't know a thing about where Frank is, and Coretta's dead."

"Dead?" She sounded as if she was really surprised.

"Yeah, they think it happened Thursday night."

"This is terrible. Do you think maybe something 'as 'appened with Frank?"

"Listen, lady, I don't know what's goin' on with Frank or anybody else. All I know is that it ain't none'a my business and I hope you do okay but I have to go right now . . ."

"But you must help me."

"No thanks, honey. This is too much fo' me."

"But if you do not help I will 'ave to go to the police to find my friend. I will 'ave to tell them about you and this woman, this Coretta."

"Listen, it was prob'ly your friend that killed her."

"She was stabbed?"

"No," I said, realizing what she meant. "She was beaten to death."

"That ees not Frank. He 'as the knife. He does not use his fists. You will help me?"

"Help you what?" I said. I put up my hands to show how helpless I was but no one could see me.

"I 'ave a friend, yes? He may know where to find Frank."

"I don't need to go lookin' fo' Frank Green but if you want'im why don't you just call this friend?"

"I, I must go to him. He 'as something for me and . . ."

"So why do you need me? If he's your friend just go to his house. Take a taxi."

"I do not 'ave the money and Frank 'as my car. It is far away, my friend's house, but I could tell you 'ow to go."

"No thanks, lady."

"Please help me. I do not want to call the police but I 'ave no other way if you do not help."

I was afraid of the police too. Afraid that the next time I went down to the police station I wouldn't be getting out. I was missing my catfish more and more. I could almost smell it frying; I could almost taste it.

"Where are you?" I asked.

"At my house, on Dinker Street. Thirty-four fifty-one and a 'alf."

"That's not where Frank lives."

"I 'ave my own place. Yes? He is not my lover."

"I could bring you some money and put you in a cab over on Main. That's all."

"Oh yes, yes! That would be fine."

At four in the morning the neighbor-hoods of Los Angeles are asleep. On Dinker Street there wasn't even a dog out prowling the trash. The dark lawns were quiet, dotted now and then with hushed white flowers that barely shone in the lamplight.

The French girl's address was a one-story duplex; the porch light shone on her half of the porch.

I stayed in my car long enough to light up a cigarette. The house looked peaceful enough. There was a fat palm tree in the front yard. The lawn was surrounded by an ornamental white picket fence. There were no bodies lying around, no hard-look-ing men with knives on the front porch. I should have taken Odell's advice right then and left California for good.

When I got to the door she was waiting behind it.

"Mr. Rawlins?"

"Easy, call me Easy."

"Oh, yes. That is what Coretta called you. Yes?"

"Yeah."

"I am Daphne, please to come in."

It was one of those houses that used to be for one family but something happened. Maybe a brother and sister inherited it and couldn't come to a deal so they just walled the place in half and called it a duplex.

She led me into the half living room. It had brown carpets, a brown sofa with a matching chair, and brown walls. There was a bushy potted fern next to the brown curtains that were closed over the entire front wall. Only the coffee table wasn't brown. It was a gilded stand on which lay a clear glass tabletop.

"A drink, Mr. Rawlins?" Her dress was the simple blue kind that the French girls wore when I was a GI in Paris. It was plain and came down to just below her knee. Her only jewelry was a small ceramic pin, worn over her left breast.

"No thanks."

Her face was beautiful. More beautiful than the photograph. Wavy hair so light brown that you might have called it blond from a distance, and eyes that were either green or blue depending on how she held her head. Her cheekbones were high but her face was full enough that it didn't make her seem severe. Her eyes were just a little closer than most women's eyes; it made her seem vulnerable, made me feel that I wanted to put my arms around her—to protect her.

We looked at each other for a few moments before she spoke. "Would you 'ave something to eat?"

"No thanks." I realized that we were whispering and asked, "Is there anybody else here?"

"No," she whispered, moving close enough for me to smell the soap she used, Ivory. "I live alone."

Then she reached out a long delicate hand to touch my face.

"You 'ave been fighting?"

"What?"

"The bruises on your face."

"Nuthin'."

She didn't move her hand.

"I could clean them for you?"

I put my hand out to touch her face, thinking, This is crazy.

"It's okay," I said. "I brought you twenty-five dollars."

She smiled like a child. Only a child could ever be that happy.

"Thank you," she said. She turned away and seated herself on the brown chair, clasping her hands on her lap. She nodded at the couch and I lowered myself.

"I got the money right here." I went for my pocket but she stopped me with a gesture.

"Couldn't you take me to him? I'm just a girl, you know. You could stay in the car and I would only take a little time. Five minutes maybe."

"Listen, honey, I don't even know you . . ."

"But I need 'elp." She looked down at the knot of hands and said, "You do not want to be bother by the police. I do not either . . ."

I'd heard that line before. "Why don't you just take the taxi?"

"I am afraid."

"But why you gonna trust me?"

"I 'ave no choice. I am a stranger 'ere and my friend is gone. When Coretta tells me that you are looking for me I ask her if you are a bad man and she says no to me. She says that you are a good man and that you are just looking, how you say, innocent."

"I just heard about ya," I said. "That's all. Bouncer at John's said that you were something to see."

She smiled for me. "You will help me, yes?"

The time for me to say no was over. If I was going to say no, it should have been to DeWitt Albright or even to Coretta. But I still had a question to ask.

"How'd you know where to call me?"

Daphne looked down at her hands for maybe three seconds; long enough for the average person to formulate a lie.

"Before I gave Coretta her money I said that I wanted to 'ave it, so I could talk to you. I wanted to know why you look for me."

She was just a girl. Nothing over twenty-two.

"Where you say your friend lives?"

"On a street above Hollywood, Laurel Canyon Road."

"You know how to get there?"

She nodded eagerly and then jumped up saying, "Just let me get one thing."

She ran out of the living room into a darkened doorway and returned in less than a minute. She was carrying an old beaten-up suitcase.

"It is Richard's, my friend's," she smiled shyly.


I drove across town to La Brea then straight north to Hollywood. The canyon road was narrow and winding but there was no traffic at all. We hadn't even seen a police car on the ride and that was fine with me, because the police have white slavery on the brain when it comes to colored men and white women.

At every other curve, near the top of the road, we'd catch a glimpse of nighttime L.A. Even way back then the city was a sea of lights. Bright and shiny and alive. Just to look out on Los Angeles at night gave me a sense of power.

"It is the next one, Easy. The one with the carport."

It was another small house. Compared with some of the mansions we'd seen on the ride it was like a servant's house. A shabby little A-frame with two windows and a gaping front door.

"Your friend always leave his door open like that?" I asked.

"I do not know."

When we parked I got out of the car with her.

"I will only be a moment." She caressed my arm before turning toward the house.

"Maybe I better go with ya."

"No," she said with strength that she hadn't shown before.

"Listen. This is late at night, in a lonely neighborhood, in a big city. That door is open and that means something's wrong. And if something happens to one more person I know the police are gonna chase me down into the grave."

"Okay," she said. "But only to see if it is alright. Then you go back to the car."

I closed the front door before turning on the wall switch. Daphne called out, "Richard!"

It was one of those houses that was designed to be a mountain cabin. The front door opened into a big room that was living room, dining room, and kitchen all in one. The kitchen was separated from the dining area by a long counter. The far left of the room had a wooden couch with a Mexican rug thrown across it and a metal chair with tan cushions for the seat and back. The wall opposite the front door was all glass. You could see the city lights winking inside the mirror image of the room, Daphne, and me.

At the far left wall was a door.

"His bedroom," she said.

The bedroom was also simple. Wood floor, window for a wall, and a king-sized bed with a dead man on it.

He was in the same blue suit. He lay across the bed, his arms out like Jesus Christ—but the fingers were jangled, not composed like they were on my mother's crucifix. He didn't call me "colored brother" but I recognized the drunken white man I'd met in front of John's place.

Daphne gasped. She grabbed my sleeve. "It is Richard."

There was a butcher's knife buried deep in his chest. The smooth brown haft stood out from his body like a cattail from a pond. He'd fallen with his back on a bunch of blankets so that the blood had flown upwards, around his face and neck. There was a lot of blood around his wide-eyed stare. Blue eyes and brown hair and dark blood so thick that you could have dished it up like Jell-O. My tongue grew a full beard and I gagged.

The next thing I knew I was down on one knee but I kept myself from being sick. I kneeled there in front of that dead man like a priest blessing a corpse brought to him by grieving relatives. I didn't know his family name or what he had done, I only knew that he was dead.

All the dead men that I'd ever known came back to me in that instant. Bernard Hooks, Addison Sherry, Alphonso Jones, Marcel Montague. And a thousand Germans named Heinz, and children and women too. Some were mutilated, some burned. I'd killed my share of them and I'd done worse things than that in the heat of war. I'd seen open-eyed corpses like this man Richard and corpses that had no heads at all. Death wasn't new to me and I was to be damned if I'd let one more dead white man break me down.

While I was down there, on my knees, I noticed something. I bent down and smelled it and then I picked it up and wrapped it in my handkerchief.

When I got to my feet I saw that Daphne was gone. I went to the kitchen and rinsed my face in the sink. I figured that Daphne had run to the toilet. But when I was through she hadn't returned. I looked in the bathroom but she wasn't there. I ran outside to look at my car but she was nowhere to be seen.

Then I heard a ruckus from the carport.

Daphne was there pushing the old suitcase into the trunk of a pink Studebaker.

"What's goin' on?" I asked.

"What'a ya think's goin' on! We gotta get out of here and it's best if we split."

I didn't have the time to wonder at her loss of accent. "What happened here?"

"Help me with my bag!"

"What happened?" I asked again.

"How the hell do I know? Richard's dead, Frank's gone too. All I know is that I have to get out of here and you better too, unless you want the police to prove you did it."

"Who did it?" I grabbed her and turned her away from the car.

"I do not know," she said quietly and calmly into my face. Our faces were no more than two inches apart.

"I cain't just leave it like this."

"There's nothing else to do, Easy. I'll take these things so nobody will know that I was ever here and you just go on home. Go to sleep and treat it like a dream."

"What about him?" I yelled, pointing at the house.

"That's a dead man, Mr. Rawlins. He's dead and gone. You just go home and forget what you saw. The police don't know you were here and they won't know unless you shout so loud that someone looks out here and sees your car."

"What you gonna do?"

"Drive his car to a little place I know and leave it there. Get on a bus for somewhere more than a thousand miles from here."

"What about the men lookin' for you?"

"You mean Carter? He doesn't mean any harm. He'll give up when they can't find me." She smiled.

Then she kissed me.

It was a slow, deliberate kiss. At first I tried to pull away but she held on strong. Her tongue moved around under mine and between my gums and lips. The bitter taste in my mouth turned almost sweet from hers. She leaned back and smiled at me for a moment and then she kissed me again. This time it was fierce. She lunged so deep into my throat that once our teeth collided and my canine chipped.

"Too bad we won't have a chance to get to know each other, Easy. Otherwise I'd let you eat this little white girl up."

"You can't just go," I stammered. "That's murder there."

She slammed the trunk shut and went around me to the driver's side of the car. She got in and rolled down the window.

"Bye, Easy," she said as she popped the ignition and threw it into reverse.

The engine choked twice but not enough to stall.

I could have grabbed her and pulled her out of the car but what would I have done with her? All I could do was watch the red lights recede down the hill.

Then I got into my car thinking that my luck hadn't turned yet.

**14**

"You lettin' them step on you, Easy. Lettin' them walk all over you and you ain't doin' a thing."

"What can I do?"

I pulled onto Sunset Boulevard and turned left, toward the band of fiery orange light on the eastern horizon.

"I don't know, man, but you gotta do somethin'. This keep up and you be dead 'fore next Wednesday."

"Maybe I should just do like Odell says and leave."

"Leave! Leave? You gonna run away from the only piece'a property you ever had? Leave," he said disgustedly. "Better be dead than leave."

"Well, you say I'ma be dead anyway. All I gotta do is wait fo' nex Wednesday."

"You gotta stand up, man. Lettin' these people step on you

ain't right. Messin' with French white girls, who ain't French; workin' fo' a white man kill his own kind if they don't smell right. You gotta find out what happened an' set it straight."

"But what can I do with the police or Mr. Albright or even that girl?"

"Bide yo' time, Easy. Don't do nuthin' that you don't have to do. Just bide yo' time an' take advantage whenever you can."

"What if . . ."

"Don't ask no questions. Either somethin' is or it ain't. 'What if' is fo' chirren, Easy. You's a man."

"Yeah," I said. Suddenly I felt stronger.

"Not too many people wanna take down a man, Easy. They's too many cowards around for that."

The voice only comes to me at the worst times, when everything seems so bad that I want to take my car and drive it into a wall. Then this voice comes to me and gives me the best advice I ever get.

The voice is hard. It never cares if I'm scared or in danger. It just looks at all the facts and tells me what I need to do.


The voice first came to me in the army.

When I joined up I was proud because I believed what they said in the papers and newsreels. I believed that I was a part of the hope of the world. But then I found that the army was segregated just like the South. They trained me as a foot soldier, a fighter, then they put me in front of a typewriter for the first three years of my tour. I had gone through Africa and Italy in the statistics unit. We followed the fighting men, tracing their movements and counting their dead.

I was in a black division but all the superior officers were white. I was trained how to kill men but white men weren't anxious to see a gun in my hands. They didn't want to see me spill white blood. They said we didn't have the discipline or the minds for a war effort, but they were really scared that we might get to like the kind of freedom that death-dealing brings.

If a black man wanted to fight he had to volunteer. Then maybe he'd get to fight.

I thought the men who volunteered for combat were fools.

"Why I wanna die in this white man's war?" I'd say.

But then one day I was in the PX when a load of white soldiers came in, fresh from battle outside Rome. They made a comment about the Negro soldiers. They said that we were cowards and that it was the white boys that were saving Europe. I knew they were jealous because we were behind the lines with good food and conquered women, but it got to me somehow. I hated those white soldiers and my own cowardice.

So I volunteered for the invasion of Normandy and then later I signed on with Patton at the Battle of the Bulge. By that time the Allies were so desperate that they didn't have the luxury of segregating the troops. There were blacks, whites, and even a handful of Japanese-Americans in our platoon. And the major thing we had to worry about was killing Germans. There was always trouble between the races, especially when it came to the women, but we learned to respect each other out there too.

I never minded that those white boys hated me, but if they didn't respect me I was ready to fight.

It was outside Normandy, near a little farm, when the voice first came to me. I was trapped in the barn. My two buddies, Anthony Yakimoto and Wenton Niles, were dead and a sniper had the place covered. The voice told me to "get off yo' butt when the sun comes down an' kill that motherfucker. Kill him an' rip off his fuckin' face with yo' bayonet, man. You cain't let him do that to you. Even if he lets you live you be scared the rest'a yo' life. Kill that motherfucker," he told me. And I did.

The voice has no lust. He never told me to rape or steal. He just tells me how it is if I want to survive. Survive like a man.

When the voice speaks, I listen.

**T**here was another car parked in front of my house when I got home. A white Cadillac. No one was in it but this time it was my front door that was open.

Manny and Shariff were loitering just inside the door. Shariff grinned at me. Manny looked at the floor so I still couldn't tell about his eyes.

Mr. Albright was standing in the kitchen, looking out over the backyards through the window. The smell of coffee filled the house. When I came in he turned to me, a porcelain cup cradled in his right hand. He wore white cotton pants and a cream sweater, white golf shoes, and a captain's cap with a black brim.

"Easy." His smile was loose and friendly.

"What you doin' in my house, man?"

"I had to talk to you. You know I expected you to be home."

There was the slightest hint of threat in his voice. "So Manny used a screwdriver on the door, just to be comfortable. Coffee's made."

"You got no excuse to be breakin' into my house, Mr. Albright. What would you do if I broke into your place?"

"I'd tear your nigger head out by its root." His smile didn't alter in the least.

I looked at him a minute. Somewhere in the back of my mind I thought, Bide your time, Easy.

"So what you want?" I asked him. I went to the counter and poured a cup of coffee.

"Where have you been this time of morning, Easy?"

"Nowhere got to do with your business."

"Where?"

I turned to him saying, "I went to see a girl. Don't you git none, Mr. Albright?"

His dead eyes turned colder and the smile left his face. I was trying to say something that would get under his skin and then I was sorry I had.

"I didn't come here to play with you, boy," he said evenly. "You got my money in your pocket and all I got is an earful of smartass."

"What do you mean?" I stopped myself from taking a step backward.

"I mean, Frank Green hasn't been home in two days. I mean that the superintendent at the Skyler Arms tells me that the police have been around his place asking about a colored girl that was seen with Green a few days before she died. I want to know, Easy. I want to know where the white girl is."

"You don't think I did my job? Shit, I give you the money back."

"Too late for that, Mr. Rawlins. You take my money and you belong to me."

"I don't belong to anybody."

"We all owe out something, Easy. When you owe out then you're in debt and when you're in debt then you can't be your own man. That's capitalism."

"I got your money right here, Mr. Albright." I reached for my pocket.

"Do you believe in God, Mr. Rawlins?"

"What do ya want, man?"

"I want to know if you believe in God."

"This here is bullshit. I gotta go to bed." I made like I was going to turn away but I didn't. I would have never knowingly turned my back on DeWitt Albright.

"Because you see," he continued, leaning slightly toward me, "I like to look very close at a man I kill if he believes in God. I want to see if death is different for a religious man."

"Bide your time," the voice whispered.

"I seen her," I said.

I went to the chair in the living room. Sitting down took a great weight off me.

Albright's henchmen moved close to me. They were roused, like hunting dogs expecting blood.

"Where?" DeWitt smiled. His eyes looked like those of the undead.

"She called me. Said that if I didn't help her she'd tell the police about Coretta . . ."

"Coretta?"

"A dead girl, friend'a mine. She prob'ly the one that the police askin' 'bout. She the one was with Frank an' your girl," I said. "Daphne gave me an address over on Dinker and I went there. Then she had me drive up in the Hollywood Hills to a dude's house."

"When was all this?"

"I just got back."

"Where is she?"

"She took off."

"Where is she?" His voice sounded as if it came from out of a well. It sounded dangerous and wild.

"I don't know! When we found the body she split in his car!"

"What body?"

"Dude was dead when we got there."

"What was this guy's name?"

"Richard."

"Richard what?"

"She just called him Richard, that's all." I saw no reason to tell him that Richard had been nosing around John's place.

"You sure he was dead?"

"Had a knife right through his chest. There was a fly marchin' right across his eye." I felt bile in my throat remembering it. "Blood everywhere."

"And you just let her go?" The threat in his voice was back so I got up and moved toward the kitchen for more coffee. I was so worried about one of them coming behind me that I bumped into the doorjamb trying to get through the door.

"Bide your time," the voice whispered again.

"You din't hire me fo' no kidnappin'. The girl grabbed his keys and split. What you want me to do?"

"You call the cops?"

"I tried my best to keep in the speed limit. That's all I did."

"Now I'm going to ask you something, Easy." His gaze held my eye. "And I don't want you to make any mistakes. Not right now."

"Go on."

"Did she take anything with her? A bag or a suitcase?"

"She had a ole brown suitcase. She put it in his trunk."

DeWitt's eyes brightened and all the tension went out of his shoulders. "What kind of car was that?"

"Forty-eight Studebaker. Pink job."

"Where'd she go? Remember, now, you're still telling me everything."

"All she said was she was gonna park it somewheres, but she didn't say where."

"What's that address she was at?"

"Twenty-six—"

He waved at me impatiently and, to my shame, I flinched.

"Write it down," he said.

I got paper from the drawer of my end table.

He sat across from me on the couch scrutinizing that little slip of paper. He had his knees wide apart.

"Get me some whiskey, Easy," he said.

"Get it yourself," the voice said.

"Get it yourself," I said. "Bottle's in the cabinet."

DeWitt Albright looked up at me, and a big grin slowly spread across his face. He laughed and slapped his knee and said, "Well, I'll be damned."

I just looked at him. I was ready to die but I was going to go down fighting.

"Get us a drink, will you, Manny?" The little man moved quickly to the cabinet. "You know, Easy, you're a brave man. And I need a brave man working for me." His drawl got thicker as he talked. "I've already paid you, right?"

I nodded.

"Well, the way I figure it, Frank Green is the key. She will be around him or he will know where she's gone to. So I want you to find this gangster for me. I want you to set me up to meet him. That's all. Once I meet him then I'll know what to say. You find Frank Green for me and we're quits."

"Quits?"

"*All* our business, Easy. You keep your money and I leave you alone."

It wasn't an offer at all. Somehow I knew that Mr. Albright planned to kill me. Either he'd kill me right then or he'd wait until I found Frank.

"I'll find him for ya, but I need another hundred if you want my neck out there."

"You my kinda people, Easy, you sure are," he said. "I'll give you three days to find him. Make sure you count them right."

We finished our drinks with Manny and Sheriff waiting outside the door.

Albright pushed open the screen to leave but then he had a thought. He turned back to me and said, "I'm not a man to fool with, Mr. Rawlins."

No, I thought to myself, neither am I.

slept all that day and into the evening. Maybe I should have been looking for Frank Green but all I wanted was to sleep.

I woke up sweating in the middle of the night. Every sound I heard was someone coming after me. Either it was the police or DeWitt Albright or Frank Green. I couldn't throw off the smell of blood that I'd picked up in Richard's room. There was the hum of a million flies at the window, flies that I'd seen swarming on our boys' corpses in North Africa, in Oran.

I was shivering but I wasn't cold. And I wanted to run to my mother or someone to love me, but then I imagined Frank Green pulling me from a loving woman's arms; he had his knife poised to press into my heart.

Finally I jumped up from my bed and ran to the telephone. I didn't know what I was doing. I couldn't call Joppy because he

wouldn't understand that kind of fear. I couldn't call Odell because he'd understand it too well and just tell me to run. I
couldn't call Dupree because he was still locked up. But I couldn't
have talked to him anyway because I would have had to lie to him
about Coretta and I was too upset to lie.

So I dialed the operator. And when she came on the line I
asked her for long distance, and then I asked for Mrs. E. Alexander on Claxton Street in Houston's Fifth Ward.

When she answered the phone I closed my eyes and remembered her: big woman with deep brown skin and topaz eyes. I
imagined her frown when she said "Hello?," because EttaMae
never liked the telephone. She always said, "I like to see my bad
news comin'; not get it like a sneak through no phones."

"Hello," she said.

"Etta?"

"Who's this?"

"It's Easy, Etta."

"Easy Rawlins?" And then a big laugh. The kind of laugh that
makes you want to laugh along with it. "Easy, where are you,
honey? You come home?"

"I'm in L.A., Etta." My voice was quavering; my chest vibrated
with feeling.

"Sumpin' wrong, honey? You sound funny."

"Uh . . . Naw, ain't nuthin', Etta. Sure is good to hear you.
Yeah, I can't think of nuthin' better."

"What's wrong, Easy?"

"You know how I can reach Mouse, Etta?"

There was silence then. I thought of how they said in science
class that outer space was empty, black and cold. I felt it then and
I sure didn't want to.

"You know Raymond and me broke up, Easy. He don't live
here no more."

The idea that I made Etta sad was almost more than I could
take.

"I'm sorry, baby," I said. "I just thought you might know how I could get to him."

"What's wrong, Easy?"

"It's just that maybe Sophie was right."

"Sophie Anderson?"

"Yeah, well, you know that she's always sayin' that L.A. is too much?"

Etta laughed in her chest. "I sure do."

"She might just be right." I laughed too.

"Easy . . ."

"Just tell Mouse that I called, Etta. Tell him that Sophie might have been right about California and maybe it is a place for him."

She started to say something else but I made like I didn't hear her and said, "Goodbye." I pushed down the button of the receiver.

I put my chair in front of the window so I could look out into my yard. I sat there for a long time, balling my hands together and taking deep breaths when I could remember to. Finally the fear passed and I fell asleep. The last thing I remember was looking at my apple tree in the pre-dawn.

I put the card that DeWitt Albright had given me on the dresser. It read:

**MAXIM BAXTER**
*Personnel Director*
*Lion Investments*

In the lower right-hand corner there was an address on La Cienega Boulevard.

I was dressed in my best suit and ready to ride by 10 A.M. I thought that it was time to gather my own information. That card was the one of two things I had to go on, so I drove across town again to a small office building just below Melrose, on La Cienega. The whole building was occupied by Lion Investments.

The secretary, an elderly lady with blue hair, was concentrating on the ledger at her desk. When my shadow fell across her blotter she said, to the shadow, "Yes?"

"I came to see Mr. Baxter."

"Do you have an appointment?"

"No. But Mr. Albright gave me his card and told me to come down whenever I had a chance."

"I know no Mr. Albright," she said, again to the shadow on her desk. "And Mr. Baxter is a very busy man."

"Maybe he knows Mr. Albright. He gave me this card." I tossed the card down onto the page she was reading and she looked up.

What she saw surprised her. "Oh!"

I smiled back down. "I can wait if he's busy. I got a little time off'a work."

"I, ah . . . I'll see if he can make time, Mr.—?"

"Rawlins."

"You just have a seat over on the couch and I'll be right back."

She went through a doorway behind the desk. After a few minutes another elderly lady came out. She looked at me suspiciously and then took up the work that the other one had left.

The waiting room was nice enough. There was a long, black leather couch set up against a window that looked out onto La Cienega Boulevard. Through the window was a view of one of those fancy restaurants, the Angus Steak House. There was a man standing out front in a Beefeater's uniform, ready to open the door for all the nice people who were going to drop a whole day's salary in forty-five minutes. The Beefeater looked happy. I wondered how much he made in tips.

There was a long coffee table in front of the couch. It was covered with business newspapers and business magazines. Nothing for women. And nothing for men who might have been looking for something sporty or entertaining. When I got tired of watching the Beefeater open doors I started looking around the room.

On the wall next to the couch was a bronze placard. At the top there was a raised oval that had the form of a swooping falcon carved into it. The falcon had three arrows in its talons. Below that were the names of all the important partners and affiliates of Lion Investments. I recognized some of the names as celebrities that you read about in the daily *Times*. Lawyers, bankers, and just the plain old wealthy folks. The president's name was at the bottom of the plaque as if he were a shy man who didn't want his name placed too obviously as the one in charge. Mr. Todd Carter wasn't the kind of man who wanted his name spread around, I figured. I mean, what would he say if he knew that a strange French girl, who went in the night to steal a dead man's car, was using his name? I laughed loud enough for the old woman behind the desk to look up and scowl.

"Mr. Rawlins," the first secretary said as she walked up to me. "You know Mr. Baxter is a very busy man. He doesn't have a lot of time . . ."

"Well, then maybe he better see me quick so he can get back to work."

She didn't like that.

"May I ask what is the nature of your request?"

"Sure you can, but I don't think your boss wants me to talk to the help about his business."

"I assure you, sir," she said, barely holding in her anger, "that whatever you have to say to Mr. Baxter is safe with me. Also, he cannot see you and I am the only person with whom you may speak."

"Naw."

"I'm afraid so. Now if you have some sort of message please tell me so I can get back to my work." She produced a small pad and a yellow, wooden pencil.

"Well, Miss—?" For some reason I thought that it would be nice if we traded names.

"What is your message, sir?"

"I see," I said. "Well, my message is this: I have news for a Mr. Todd Carter, the president of your company, I believe. I was given Mr. Baxter's card to forward a message to Mr. Carter about a job I was employed to do by a Mr. DeWitt Albright." I stopped there.

"Yes? What job is that?"

"Are you sure you want to know?" I asked.

"What job, sir?" If she was nervous at all I couldn't see it.

"Mr. Albright hired me to find Mr. Carter's girlfriend after she ditched him."

She stopped writing and peered at me over the rim of her bifocals. "Is this some sort of joke?"

"Not that I know of, ma'am. As a matter of fact, I haven't had a good laugh since I went to work for your boss. Not one laugh at all."

"Excuse me," she said.

She slammed the pad down hard enough to startle her helper and disappeared through the back door again.

She wasn't gone for more than five minutes when a tall man in a dark gray suit came out to see me. He was thin with bushy black hair and thick black eyebrows. His eyes seemed to pull back into shadows under those hefty brows.

"Mr. Rawlins." His smile was so white that it would have looked at home on DeWitt Albright.

"Mr. Baxter?" I rose and grabbed his extended hand.

"Why don't you come with me, sir?"

We went past the two scowling women. I was sure that they'd put their heads together and start gabbing as soon as Mr. Baxter and I had gone through the door.

The hallway we entered was narrow but well carpeted and the walls were papered with a plush blue fabric. At the end of the hall was a fine oak door with "Maxim T. Baxter, Vice-President," carved into it.

His office was modest and small. The ash desk was good but not big or fancy. The floor was pine and the window behind his desk looked out onto a parking lot.

"Not very smart talking about Mr. Carter's business to the front desk," Baxter said the moment we were both seated.

"I don't wanna hear it, man."

"What?" It was a question but there was a kind of superiority in his tone.

"I said I don't wanna hear it, Mr. Baxter. It's just too much goin' on fo' me t'be worried 'bout what you think ain't right. Ya see, if you'd let that woman out there know that she should let me talk to you, then—"

"I *asked* her to get a message from you, Mr. Rawlins. It is my understanding that you're looking for employment. I could set up an appointment for you through the mails . . ."

"I'm here to talk to Mr. Carter."

"That's impossible," he said. Then he stood up as if that would scare me.

I looked up at him and said, "Man, why don't you sit down and get your boss on the line."

"I don't know who you think you are, Rawlins. Important men don't even barge in on Mr. Carter. You're lucky that I took the time to see you."

"You mean the poor nigger lucky the foreman take out the time t'curse'im, huh?"

Mr. Baxter looked at his watch instead of answering me. "I have an appointment, Mr. Rawlins. If you just tell me what you want to say to Mr. Carter he'll call you if it seems appropriate."

"That's what the lady out there said, and you go blamin' me for shootin' off my mouth."

"I'm aware of Mr. Carter's situation; the ladies outside are not."

"You might be aware of what he told you but you ain't got no idea of what I gotta say."

"And what might that be?" he asked, sitting back down.

"All I'm'a tell ya is that he might be runnin' Lion from a jail cell if he don't speak to me, and real quick too." I didn't exactly know what I meant but it shook up Baxter enough for him to pick up his phone.

"Mr. Carter," he said. "Mr. Albright's operative is here and he wants to see you . . . Albright, the man we have on the Monet thing . . . He sounds as though it's urgent, sir. Maybe you should see him . . ."

They talked a little more but that was the gist of it.

Baxter led me back down the hall but made a left turn before we went through the door that led to the secretaries. We came to a darkwood door that was locked. Baxter had a key for it and when he pulled it open I saw that it was the door to a tiny, padded elevator.

"Get in, it will take you to his office," Baxter said.


There was no feeling of motion, only the soft hum of a motor somewhere below the floor. The elevator had a bench and an ashtray. The walls and ceiling were covered in velvety red fabric that was cut into squares. Each square had a pair of dancing figures in it. The waltzing men and women were dressed like courtiers of the French court. The wealth made my heart beat fast.

The door came open on a small, red-headed man who wore a tan suit that he might have bought at Sears Roebuck and a simple white shirt that was open at the collar. At first I thought he was Mr. Carter's servant but then I realized that we were the only ones in the room.

"Mr. Rawlins?" He fingered his receding hairline and shook my hand. His grip felt like paper. He was so small and quiet that he seemed more like a child than a man.

"Mr. Carter. I came to tell you—"

He put up a hand and shook his head before I could go on.

Then he led me across the wide room to the pair of pink couches that stood in front of his desk. The desk was the color and size of a grand piano. The great brocade curtains behind the desk were open to a view of the mountains behind Sunset Boulevard.

I remember thinking that it was a long way from vice-president to the top.

We sat at either end of one of the couches.

"Drink?" He pointed at a crystal decanter that held a brown liquid on an end table near me.

"What is it?" My voice sounded strange in the large room.

"Brandy."

That was the first time I ever had really good liquor. I liked it just fine.

"Mr. Baxter said that you had news from that man Albright."

"Well, not exactly, sir."

He frowned when I said that. It was a little boy's frown; it made me feel sorry for him.

"You see, I'm a little unhappy about how things are going with Mr. Albright. As a matter of fact, I'm unhappy about almost everything that's happened to me since I met the man."

"And what's that?"

"A woman, a friend of mine, was killed when she started asking questions about Miss Monet and the police think I had something to do with it. I've been mixed up with hijackers and wild people all over town and all because I asked a couple'a questions about your friend."

"Has anything happened to Daphne?"

He looked so worried that I was happy to say, "The last time I saw her she looked just fine."

"You saw her?"

"Yeah. Night before last."

Tears welled up in his pale, child's eyes.

"What did she say?" he asked.

"We were in trouble, Mr. Carter. But you see that's how it's crazy. The first time I saw her she was talking like she was a French girl. But then, after we found the body, she sounded like she could have come from San Diego or anywhere else."

"Body? What body?"

"I'm'a get to that but first we got to come to some kinda understanding."

"You want money."

"Uh-uh, no. I been paid already an' I guess that comes from you anyway. But what I need is for you to help me understand what's happening. You see, I don't trust your man Albright at all and you can forget the police. I got this one friend, Joppy, but this is too much for him. So I figure you the only one can help. I gotta figure that you want the girl 'cause you love'er and if I'm wrong 'bout that then my ass is had."

"I love Daphne," he said.

I was almost embarrassed to hear him. He wasn't trying to act like a man at all. He was wringing his hands trying to keep from asking about her while I talked.

"Then you gotta tell me why Albright is lookin' for her."

Carter ran his finger along his hairline again and looked out at the mountains. He waited another moment before saying, "I was told, by a man I trust, that Mr. Albright is good at doing things, confidentially. There are reasons that I don't want this affair in the papers."

"You married?"

"No, I want to marry Daphne."

"She didn't steal anything from you?"

"Why do you ask?"

"Mr. Albright seems real concerned about her luggage and I thought she had something you wanted back."

"You might call it stealing, Mr. Rawlins, it doesn't matter to me. She took some money when she left but I don't care about that. I want her. You say she was fine when you saw her?"

"How much money?"

"I don't see where that matters."

"If you want me to answer questions then you give too."

"Thirty thousand dollars." He said it as if it was just some pocket change on the bathroom shelf. "I had it at home because we were giving the people in our various concerns half-a-day holiday as a sort of bonus but the day we chose was a payday and the bank couldn't deliver the cash that early so I had them deliver it to my home."

"You let the bank deliver that much money to your house?"

"It was only once, and what were the odds I'd be robbed that night?"

"About one hundred percent, I guess."

He smiled. "The money means nothing to me. Daphne and I had a fight and she took the money because she thought I'd never talk to her again. She was wrong."

"Fight about what?"

"They tried to blackmail her. She came to me and told me about it. They wanted to use her to get at me. She made up her mind to leave, to save me."

"What they got on her?"

"I'd rather not say."

I let it pass. "Albright know about the money?"

"Yes. Now I've answered your questions, I want to know about her. Is she all right?"

"Last I saw of her she was fine. She was looking for her friend—Frank Green."

I thought that a man's name might shake him up but Todd Carter didn't even seem to hear it. "What did you say about a body?"

"We went to another friend of hers, a man named Richard, and we found him dead in his bed."

"Richard McGee?" Carter's voice went cold.

"I don't know. All I know is Richard."

"Did he live on Laurel Canyon Road?"

"Yeah."

"Good. I'm glad he's dead. I'm glad. He was an awful man. Did she tell you that he dealt in young boys?"

"All she said was that he was a friend'a hers."

"Well he did. He was a blackmailer and a homosexual pimp. He worked for rich men with sick appetites."

"Well he's dead and Daphne took his car, that was night before last. She said that she was gonna leave the city. That was the last I heard of her."

"What was she wearing?" His eyes were glistening, expectant.

"A blue dress and blue heels."

"Was she wearing stockings?"

"I think so." I didn't want him to think I was looking too closely.

"What color?"

"Blue too, I think."

He smiled with all his teeth. "That's her. Tell me, did she wear a pin here, on her chest?"

"On the other side, but yeah. It was red with little green dots in it."

"You want another drink, Mr. Rawlins?"

"Sure."

He poured that time.

"She's a beautiful woman, isn't she?"

"You wouldn't be lookin' for her if she wasn't."

"I never knew a woman who could wear perfume where the smell was so slight that you just wanted to get closer to tell what it was."

Ivory soap, I thought to myself.

He asked me about her makeup and her hair. He told me that she was from New Orleans and that her family was an old French family that traced their heritage to Napoleon. We talked about her eyes for a half hour. And then he started to tell me things that men should never say about their women. Not sex, but he talked about how she'd hold him to her breast when he was afraid and how she'd stand up for him when a shopkeeper or waiter tried to walk over him.

Talking with Mr. Todd Carter was a strange experience. I mean, there I was, a Negro in a rich white man's office, talking to him like we were best friends—even closer. I could tell that he didn't have the fear or contempt that most white people showed when they dealt with me.

It was a strange experience but I had seen it before. Mr. Todd Carter was so rich that he didn't even consider me in human terms. He could tell me anything. I could have been a prized dog that he knelt to and hugged when he felt low.

It was the worst kind of racism. The fact that he didn't even recognize our difference showed that he didn't care one damn about me. But I didn't have the time to worry about it. I just watched him move his lips about lost love until, finally, I began to see him as some strange being. Like a baby who grows to man-size and terrorizes his poor parents with his strength and his stupidity.

"I love her, Mr. Rawlins. I'd do anything to get her back."

"Well I wish ya luck on that. But I think you better get Albright away from her. He wants that money."

"Will you find her for me? I'll give you a thousand dollars."

"What about Albright?"

"I'll tell my associates to fire him. He won't go against us."

"Suppose he does?"

"I'm a rich man, Mr. Rawlins. The mayor and the chief of police eat at my house regularly."

"Then why can't they help you?"

He turned away from me when I asked that.

"Find her for me," he said.

"If you gimme something to hold, say two hundred dollars, I'll give it a try. I ain't sayin' nuthin's gonna come from it. She could be back in New Orleans for all I know."

He stood up smiling. He touched my hand with his papery grip. "I'll have Mr. Baxter draw up a check."

"Uh, sorry, but I need cash."

He pulled out his wallet and flipped through the bills. "I have a hundred and seventy-some-odd in here. They could write you a check for the rest."

"I'll take one-fifty," I said.

He just took all the money from his wallet and handed it over, mumbling, "Take it all, take it all."

And I took it too.

Somewhere along the way I had developed the feeling that I wasn't going to outlive the adventure I was having. There was no way out but to run, and I couldn't run, so I decided to milk all those white people for all the money they'd let go of.

Money bought everything. Money paid the rent and fed the kitty. Money was why Coretta was dead and why DeWitt Albright was going to kill me. I got the idea, somehow, that if I got enough money then maybe I could buy my own life back.

had to find Frank Green.

Knifehand held the answer to my problems. He knew where the girl was, if anybody did, and he knew who killed Coretta; I was sure of that. Richard McGee was dead too, but I didn't care about that death because the police couldn't connect me to it.

It's not that I had no feelings for the murdered man; I thought it was wrong for a man to be murdered and, in a more perfect world, I felt that the killer should be brought to justice.

But I didn't believe that there was justice for Negroes. I thought that there might be some justice for a black man if he had the money to grease it. Money isn't a sure bet but it's the closest to God that I've ever seen in this world.

But I didn't have any money. I was poor and black and a likely candidate for the penitentiary unless I could get Frank to stand between me and the forces of DeWitt Albright and the law.

So I went out looking.

The first place I went was Ricardo's Pool Room on Slauson. Ricardo's was just a hole-in-the-wall with no windows and only one door. There was no name out front because either you knew where Ricardo's was or you didn't belong there at all.

Joppy had taken me to Ricardo's a few times after we locked up his bar. It was a serious kind of place peopled with jaundice-eyed bad men who smoked and drank heavily while they waited for a crime they could commit.

It was the kind of place you could get killed in but I was safe as long as I was with a tough man like Joppy Shag. Still, when Joppy would leave the pool table to go to the toilet I could almost feel the violence pulsing in the dark.

But I had to go to places like Ricardo's to look for Frank Green. Because Frank was in the hurting trade. Maybe there was somebody who had taken his money, or messed with his girl, and Frank needed a gunman to back him up in the kill—Ricardo's was where he'd go. Maybe he just needed an extra hand in taking down a cigarette shipment. The men in Ricardo's were desperate; they lived for hurting.

It was a large room with four pool tables, a green lamp shade hanging above each one. The walls were lined with straight-back chairs where most of the customers sat, drinking from brown paper bags and smoking in the dim light. Only one skinny youth was shooting pool. That was Mickey, Rosetta's son.

Rosetta had run the place ever since Ricardo got diabetes and lost both his legs. He was upstairs someplace, in a single bed, drinking whiskey and staring at the walls.

When I'd heard about Ricardo's illness I said to her, "I'm sorry t'hear it, Rose."

Rosetta's face was squat and wide. Her beady eyes pressed down into her chubby brown cheeks. She squinted at me and said, "He done enough ho'in 'round fo' two men and then some. I guess he could rest now." And that's all she said.

She was sitting at the only card table at the far side of the room. I walked over to her and said, "Evenin', Rosetta, how you doin' t'nite."

"Joppy here?" she asked, looking around me.

"Naw. He still workin' at the bar."

Rosetta looked at me as if I were a stray cat come in after her cheese.

The room was so dark and smoky that I couldn't make out what anyone was doing, except for Mickey, but I felt eyes on me from the haze. When I turned back to Rosetta I saw that she was staring too.

"Anybody been sellin' some good whiskey lately, Rose?" I asked. I had hoped to have some light talk with her before asking my question but her stare unsettled me and the room was too quiet for just talk.

"This ain't no bar, honey. You want whiskey you better go see yo' friend Joppy." She glanced at the door, telling me to leave, I suppose.

"I don't want a drink, Rose. I'm lookin' t'buy a case or two. Thought maybe you might know how I could get some."

"Why'ont you ast yo' friend anyway? He know where the whiskey grow."

"Joppy send me here, Rose. He say you the one t'know."

She was still suspicious but I could see that she wasn't afraid. "You could try Frank Green if you want t'buy by the box."

"Yeah? Where can I get a'hold of'im?"

"I ain't seen'im in a few days now. Either he shacked up or he out earnin' his trade."

That was all Rosetta had to say on the subject. She lit up a cigarette and turned away. I thanked her back and wandered over to Mickey.

"Eight ball?" asked Mickey.

It really didn't matter what we played. I put a five down and lost it, then I lost five more. That took me about a half an hour. When I figured I'd paid enough for my information I saluted the hustler and walked out into the sun.

I had a feeling of great joy as I walked away from Ricardo's. I don't know how to say it, exactly. It was as if for the first time in my life I was doing something on my own terms. Nobody was telling me what to do. I was acting on my own. Maybe I hadn't found Frank but I had gotten Rosetta to bring up his name. If she had known where he was I would have gotten to him that day.

There was a big house on Isabella Street, at the end of a cul-de-sac. That was Vernie's place. Lots of working men would drop by there now and then, to visit one of Vernie's girls. It was a friendly place. The second and third floors had three bedrooms each and the first floor was a kitchen and living room where the guests could be entertained.

Vernie was a light-skinned woman whose hair was frosted gold. She weighed about three hundred pounds. Vernie would stay in the kitchen cooking all day and all night. Her daughter, Darcel, who was the same size as her mother, would welcome the men into the parlor and collect a few dollars for their food and drinks.

Some men, like Odell, would be happy to sit around and drink and listen to music on the phonograph. Vernie would come out now and then to shout hello at old friends and introduce herself to newcomers.

But if you were there for companionship there were girls upstairs who sat out in front of their doors if they weren't occupied with a customer. Huey Barnes sat in the hall on the second floor. He was a wide-hipped, heavy-boned man who had the face of an innocent child. But Huey was fast and vicious despite his looks, and his presence caused all business at Vernie's to run smoothly.

I went there in the early afternoon.

"Easy Rawlins." Darcel reached her fat hands out to me. "I did believe that you had died and left us for heaven."

"Uh-uh, Darcie. You know I just been savin' it up for ya."

"Well bring it on in here, baby. Bring it on in."

She led me by the hand to the living room. A few men were sitting around drinking and listening to jazz records. There was a big bowl of dirty rice on the coffee table and white porcelain plates too.

"Easy Rawlins!" The voice came from the door to the kitchen.

"How you, baby?" Vernie asked as she ran up to me.

"Just fine, Vernie, just fine."

The big woman hugged me so that I felt I was being rolled up in a feather mattress.

"Uh," she groaned, almost lifting me from the floor. "It's been too long, honey. Too long!"

"Yeah, yeah," I said. I hugged her back and then lowered onto the couch.

Vernie smiled on me. "You stay put now, Easy. I want you to tell me how things is goin' before you go wandr'in' upstairs." And with that she went back to the kitchen.

"Hey, Ronald, what's goin' on?" I said to the man next to me.

"Not much, Ease," Ronald White answered. He was a plumber for the city. Ronald always wore his plumber's overalls no matter where he was. He said that a man's work clothes are the only real clothes he has.

"Takin' a break from all them boys?" I liked to kid Ronald about his family. His wife dropped a son every twelve or fourteen months. She was a religious woman and didn't believe in taking precautions. At the age of thirty-four Ronald had nine sons, and one on the way.

"They like to tear the place down, Easy. I swear." Ronald shook his head. "They'd be climbin' 'cross the ceilin' if they could get a good hold. You know they got me afraid to go home."

"Oh com'on now, man. It can't be that bad."

Ronald's forehead wrinkled up like a prune, and he had pain in his face when he said, "No lie, Easy. I come on in and there's a whole army of'em, runnin' right at me. First the big ones come leapin'. Then the ones can hardly walk. And while the little ones come crawlin' Mary walks in, so weak that she's like death, and she's got two babies in her arms.

"I tell ya, Easy. I spend fifty dollars on food and just watch them chirren destroy it. They eat every minute that they ain't yellin'." There were actually tears in Ronald's eyes. "I swear I can't take it, man. I swear."

"Darcel!" I yelled. "Come bring Ronald a drink, quick. You know he needs it too."

Darcel brought in a bottle of I. W. Harpers and poured all three of us a drink. I handed her three dollars for the bottle.

"Yeah," Curtis Cross said. He was sitting in front of a plate of rice at the dining table. "Chirren is the most dangerous creatures on the earth, with the exception of young girls between the ages of fifteen and forty-two."

That even got Ronald to smile.

"I don't know," Ronald said. "I love Mary but I think I'm'a have to run soon. Them kids a'kill me if I don't."

"Have another drink, man. Darcie, just keep'em comin', huh? This man needs to forget."

"You already paid for this bottle, Easy. You can waste it any way you want." Like most black women Darcel wasn't happy to hear about a man who wanted to abandon his wife and kids.

"Just three dollars and you still make some money?" I acted like I was surprised.

"We buy bulk, Easy." Darcie smiled at me.

"Could I buy it like that too," I asked, as if it was the first time I had ever heard of buying hijack.

"I don't know, honey. You know Momma and me let Huey take care of the shoppin'."

That was it for me. Huey wasn't the kind of man to ask about Frank Green. Huey was like Junior Forney—mean and spiteful. He was no one to tell my business.

I drove Ronald home at about nine. He was crying on my shoulder when I let him out at his house.

"Please don't make me go in there, Easy. Take me with you, brother."

I was trying to keep from laughing. I could see Mary at the door. She was thin except for her belly and there was a baby boy in each of her arms. All their children crowded around her in the doorway pushing each other back to get a look at their father coming home.

"Come on now, Ron. You made all them babies, now you got to sleep in your bed."

I remember thinking that if I lived through the troubles I had then, my life would be pretty good. But Ronald didn't have any chance to be happy, unless he broke his poor family's heart.

During the next day I went to the bars that Frank sold hijack to and to the alley crap games that he frequented. I never brought up Frank's name though. Frank was skitterish, like all gangsters, and if he felt that people were talking about him he got nervous; if Frank was nervous he might have killed me before I had time to make my pitch.

It was those two days more than any other time that made me a detective.

I felt a secret glee when I went into a bar and ordered a beer with money someone else had paid me. I'd ask the bartender his name and talk about anything, but, really, behind my friendly talk, I was working to find something. Nobody knew what I was up to and that made me sort of invisible; people thought that they saw me but what they really saw was an illusion of me, something that wasn't real.

I never got bored or frustrated. I wasn't even afraid of DeWitt Albright during those days. I felt, foolishly, safe from even his crazy violence.

**Z**eppo could always be found on the corner of Forty-ninth and McKinley. He was half Negro, half Italian, and palsied. He stood there looking to the world like a skinny, knotted-up minister when the word of the Lord gets in him. He'd shake and writhe with all kinds of frowns on his face. Sometimes he'd bend all the way down to the ground and place both palms on the pavement as if the street were trying to swallow him and he was pushing it away.

Ernest, the barber, let Zeppo stand out in front of his shop to beg because he knew that the neighborhood children wouldn't bother Zeppo as long as he stood in front of the barber's pane.

"Hey, Zep, how you doin'?" I asked.

"J-j-ju-j-just fi-f-f-fi-f-fine, Ease." Sometimes words would come easy to him and other times he couldn't even finish a sentence.

"Nice day, huh?"

"Y-y-y-yeah. G-go-g-g-go-good d-day," he stammered, holding his hands before his face, like claws.

"Alright," I said, and then I walked into the barbershop.

"Hey, Easy," Ernest said as he folded his newspaper and stood up from his barber's chair. I took his place and he blossomed the crisp white sheet over me, knotting the bib snug at my throat.

"I thought you come in on Thursdays, Ease?"

"Man can't always be the same, Ernest. Man gotta change with the days."

"Hotcha! Lord, give me that seven!" someone shouted from the back of the narrow shop. There was always a game of craps at the back of Ernest's shop; a group of five men were on their knees back beyond the third barber chair.

"So you looked in the mirror this mo'nin' and saw a haircut, huh?" Ernest asked me.

"Grizzly as a bear."

Ernest laughed and took a couple of practice snips with his scissors.

Ernest always played Italian opera on the radio. If you asked him why he'd just say that Zeppo like it. But Zeppo couldn't hear that radio from the street and Ernest only had him in the shop once a month, for his free haircut.

Ernest's father had been a drinking man. He beat poor little Ernest and Ernest's mother until the blood ran. So Ernest didn't have much patience with drinkers. And Zeppo was a drinker. I guess all that shaking didn't seem so bad if he had a snout full of cheap whiskey. So he'd beg until he had enough for a can of beans and a half-pint of scotch. Then Zeppo would get drunk.

It was because Zeppo was almost always drunk, or on the way to being drunk, that Ernest wouldn't allow him in the shop.

I once asked him why he'd let Zeppo hang out in front of the store if he hated drunks so much. And he told me, "The Lord might ask one day why I didn't look over my little brother."

We shot the breeze while the men threw their bones and Zeppo twisted and jerked in the window; *Don Giovanni* whispered from the radio. I wanted to find out the whereabouts of Frank Green but it had to come up in normal conversation. Most barbers know all the important information in the community. That's why I was getting my hair cut.

Ernest was brushing the hot lather around my ears when Jackson Blue came in the door.

"Happenin', Ernest, Ease," he hailed.

"Jackson," I said.

"Lenny over there, Blue," Ernest warned.

I glanced over at Lenny. He was a fat man, on his knees in a gardener's suit and a white painter's cap. He was biting a cigar butt and squinting at Jackson Blue.

"You tell that skinny bastard t'get away from here, Ernie. I kill the mothahfuckah. I ain't foolin'," Lenny warned.

"He ain't messin' wit' you, Lenny. Get back to your game or get outta my shop."

One nice thing about barbers is that they have a dozen straight razors that they will use to keep order in their shops.

"What's wrong with Lenny?" I asked.

"Just a fool," Ernest said. "Thas all. Jackson here is too."

"What happened?"

Jackson was a small man and very dark. He was so black that his skin glinted blue in the full sun. He cowered and shone his big eyes at the door.

"Lenny's girlfriend, you know Elba, left him again," Ernest said.

"Yeah?" I was wondering how to turn the conversation to Frank Green.

"And she come purrin' 'round Jackson just t'get Lenny riled."

Jackson was looking at the floor. He wore a loose, striped blue suit and small-brimmed brown felt hat.

"She did?"

"Yeah, Easy. And you know Jackson stick his business in a meat grinder if it winked at him."

"I'idn't mess wit' her. She jus' tole'im that." Jackson was pouting.

"I guess my stepbrother be lyin' too?" Lenny was right there with us. It was like a comic scene in the movies because Jackson looked scared, like a cornered dog, and Lenny, with his fat gut hanging down, was like a bully dog bearing down on him.

"Back off!" Ernest shouted, putting himself between the two men. "Any man can come in here wit'out fightin' if he wants."

"This skinny lil booze hound gonna have to answer on Elba, Ernie."

"He ain't gonna do it here. I swear you gonna have t'come through me t'get Jackson and you know he ain't worth that kinda pain."

I remembered then how Jackson sometimes made his money.

Lenny reached out at Jackson but the little man got behind Ernest and Ernest stood there, like a rock. He said, "Go back to your game while the blood still in your veins, man," then he pulled a straight razor from the pocket of his blue smock.

"You ain't got no cause to threaten me, Ernie. I ain't shit on no man's doorstep." He was moving his head back and forth trying to see Jackson behind the barber's back.

I started to get nervous sitting there between them and took off the bib. I used it to wipe the lather from my neck.

"See that, Lenny. You botherin' my customer, brother." Ernest pointed a finger thick as a railroad tie at Lenny's belly. "Either you get back in the back or I'm'a skin ya. No lie."

Anybody who knew Ernest knew that that was his last warning. You had to be tough to be a barber because your place was the center of business for a certain element in the community. Gamblers, numbers runners, and all sorts of other private businessmen met in the barbershop. The barbershop was like a social club. And any social club had to have order to run smoothly.

Lenny tucked in his chin and shifted his shoulders this way and that, then he shuffled backwards a few steps.

I got out of the chair and slapped six bits down on the counter. "There you go, Ernie," I said.

Ernie nodded in my direction but he was too busy staring Lenny down to look at me.

"Why don't we split," I said to the cowering Jackson. Whenever Jackson was nervous he'd have to touch his thing; he was holding on to it right then.

"Sure, Easy, I think Ernie got it covered here."

We turned down the first corner we came to and then down an alley, half a block away. If Lenny was to come after us he'd have to want us bad enough to hunt.

He didn't find us, but as we were walking down Merriweather Lane someone shouted, "Blue!"

It was Zeppo. He hobbled after us like a man on invisible crutches. At every step he teetered on the edge of falling over but then he'd take another step, saving himself, just barely.

"Hey, Zep," Jackson said. He was looking over Zeppo's shoulder to see if Lenny was coming.

"J-Jackson."

"What you want, Zeppo?" I wanted something from Jackson myself and I didn't need an audience.

Zeppo craned his head back further than I thought was possible, then he brought his wrists to his shoulder. He looked like a bird in agony. His smile was like death itself. "L-L-Lenny show i-is m-m-m-m-ad." Then he started coughing, which for Zeppo was a laugh. "Y-y-you-ou s-sellin', B-Blue?"

I could have kissed the cripple.

"Naw, man," Jackson said. "Frank gone big time now. He only sell by the crate to the stores. He say he don't want no nickels and dimes."

"You don't sell fo' Frank any more?" I asked.

"Uh-uh. He too big fo'a niggah like me."

"Shit! An' I was lookin' fo' some whiskey too. I gotta party in mind that need some booze."

"Well maybe I could set a deal, Ease." Jackson's eyes lit up. He was still turning now and then to see if Lenny was coming.

"Like what?"

"Maybe if you buy enough Frank'a cut us a deal."

"Like how much?"

"How much you need?"

"Case or two of Jim Beam be fine."

Jackson scratched his chin. "Frank'a sell by the case t'me. I could buy three an' sell one by the bottle."

"When you gonna see'im?" I must've sounded too eager because a caution light went on in Jackson's eye. He waited a long moment then said, "Whas up, Easy?"

"What you mean?"

"I mean," he said, "why is you lookin' fo' Frank?"

"Man, I don't know what you mean. All I know is I got people comin' to the house on Saturday and the cupboard is bare. I got a couple'a bucks but I was laid off last Monday and I can't spend it all on whiskey."

All this time Zeppo was shimmying there next to us. He was waiting to see if a bottle would materialize out of our talk.

"Yeah, well, if you need it fast," Jackson said, still suspicious, "what if I get you a deal somewhere's else?"

"I don't care. All I want is some cheap whiskey and I thought that was the business you did."

"It is, Easy. You know I usually buy from Frank but maybe I could go someplace he sells ta. Cost a little more but you still save some money."

"Anything you say, Jackson. Just lead me to the well."

"M-m-m-m-me too," Zeppo added.

When we got to my car I drove down Central to Seventy-sixth Place. I was nervous being so close to the police station but I had to find Frank Green.

Jackson took Zeppo and me down to Abe's liquor store. I was glad that Zeppo had come along with us because people who didn't know Zeppo kept their eyes and attention on him. I was banking on that to hide any questions I asked about Frank.

On the way down to the liquor store Jackson told me the story of the men that owned it.

Abe and Johnny were brothers-in-law. They came from Poland, most recently from the town of Auschwitz; Jews who survived the

Nazi camps. They were barbers in Poland and they were barbers in Auschwitz, too.

Abe was part of the underground in the camp and he saved Johnny from the gas chamber when Johnny was so sick that the Nazi guard had selected him to die. Abe dug a hole in the wall next to his bed and he put Johnny there, telling the guard that Johnny had died and was picked up, by the evening patrol, for cremation. Abe collected food from his friends in the resistance and fed his ailing brother-in-law through a hole in the wall. That went on for three months before the camp was liberated by the Russians.

Abe's wife and sister, Johnny's wife, were dead. Their parents and cousins and everyone else they had ever known or had ever been related to had died in the Nazi camps. Abe took Johnny on a stretcher and dragged him to the GI station where they applied to immigrate.

Jackson wanted to tell me more stories he'd heard about the camps but I didn't need to hear them. I remembered the Jews. Nothing more than skeletons, bleeding from their rectums and begging for food. I remembered them waving their weak hands in front of themselves, trying to keep modest; then dropping dead right there before my eyes.

Sergeant Vincent LeRoy found a twelve-year-old boy who was bald and weighed forty-six pounds. The boy ran to Vincent and hugged his leg, like the little Mexican boy clung to Matthew Teran. Vincent was a hard man, a gunner, but he melted for that little boy. He called him Tree Rat because of the way the boy crawled up on him and wouldn't let go.

The first day Vincent carried Tree Rat on his back while we evacuated the concentration camp survivors. That night he made Tree Rat go with the nurses to the evacuation center, but the little boy got away from them and made it back to our bivouac.

Vincent decided to keep him after that. Not the way Matthew Teran kept the Mexican boy, but like any man whose heart goes out to children.

Little Tree, as I called him, rode on Vincent's back all the next day. He ate a giant chocolate bar that Vincent had in his pack and other sweets the men gave him.

That night we were awakened by Tree's moaning. His little stomach had distended even more and he couldn't even hear us trying to soothe him.

The camp doctor said that he died from the richness of the food he'd been eating.

Vincent cried for a whole day after Tree Rat died. He blamed himself, and I suppose he had a share of the blame. But I'll never forget thinking how those Germans had hurt that poor boy so terribly that he couldn't even take in anything good. That was why so many Jews back then understood the American Negro; in Europe the Jew had been a Negro for more than a thousand years.

Abe and Johnny came to America and had a liquor store in less than two years. They worked hard for what they got but there was just one thing wrong: Johnny was wild.

Jackson said, "I don't know if he got like that in that hole in the wall or he was always like that. He said that he went crazy for a night, once, because him an' Abe had to cut the hair from they own wives' heads fo' they went to the gas chambers. Imagine that? Cuttin' yo' own wive's hair an' then sendin' her ta die? . . . Anyway, maybe he went crazy for the night an' now that's why he's so wild."

"What you mean, wild?" I asked him.

"Just wild, Easy. One night I goes down there with this high school girl, Donna Frank, an' I'm lookin' to impress her wit' some liquor and Abe is already gone. So Johnny acts like I'm not even there an' he start tellin' her how pretty she is an' how he'd like t'give her sumpin'."

"Yeah?"

"He give her five dollars an' had me stand at the register while he fuckin' her right there behind the counter!"

"You lyin'!"

"Naw, Easy, that boy gotta screw loose, couple of'em."

"So you go inta business then?"

"Shit no, that dude scared me. But I told Frank about it and he made the connection. You see, Frank had gone to Abe one time but Abe didn't want nuthin' t'do wit' no hijack. But Johnny love it, all he sells is hijack after Abe go home at night."

"Frank delivers here regular?" I asked.

"Yeah."

"Just like a delivery truck, huh?" I laughed. "He drive up on Wednesday afternoon an' unload."

"Us'ly it's Thursday," Jackson said, but then he frowned.

It was just a hole-in-the-wall liquor store. They had one rack for cakes, potato chips, and bagged pork rinds in the middle of the floor. There was a long candy counter and behind that were the shelves of liquor and the cash register. At the back wall was a glass-door refrigerator where they had mixers and soda pop.

Johnny was a tall man with sandy hair and glassy brown eyes. There was a look on his face halfway between a smile and wonderment. He looked like a young boy who had already gone bad.

"Hiya, Johnny," Jackson said. "This here's my friends Easy an' Zeppo."

Zeppo came twisting in behind us. Johnny's smile hardened a little when he saw Zeppo. Some people are afraid of palsy, maybe they're afraid they'll catch it.

"Good day, sirs," he said to us.

"You gonna have to start givin' me a percent, Johnny, much business as I bring you. Easy gettin' ready fo'a party an' Zeppo need his milk ev'ry day."

Johnny laughed, keeping his eyes on Zeppo. He asked, "What do you need, Easy?"

"I need a case'a Jim Beam an' Jackson say you could get it a little cheaper than normal."

"I can give it discount if you buy by the box." His accent was heavy but he understood English well enough.

"What can you do for two cases?"

"Three dollars the bottle, anywhere else you pay four."

"Yeah, that's good, but just a touch over my budget. You know I lost my job last week."

"Oh, that's too bad," Johnny said, and turned to me. "Here it is your birthday and they throw you out."

"Just a party. How 'bout two-seventy-five?"

He brought up his right hand rubbing the fingers. "I'd be giving it to you for that, my friend. But I tell you what," he said. "Two cases at three dollars is fifty-four. I let you have them for fifty."

I should have haggled for more but I was impatient to get out of there. I could tell Albright that Frank would be there Friday and on Thursday Frank and I would make a deal.

"Deal," I said. "Can I pick it up tomorrow?"

"Why can't we do business now?" he asked suspiciously.

"I ain't got no fifty dollars on me, man. I could get it by tomorrow."

"I can't do it until Friday. I have another delivery Friday."

"Why not tomorrow?" I asked just to throw him off.

"I can't sell all my whiskey to one man, Easy. Tomorrow I will get two cases but what if a customer comes in and wants Jim Beam? If I don't have it he goes to another store. Not good for business."

We settled the deal with a ten-dollar deposit. I bought Zeppo a half-pint of Harpers and I gave Jackson a five.

"Whas happenin', Easy?" Jackson said to me after Zeppo had gone off.

"Nuthin'. What you talkin' 'bout?"

"I mean you ain't givin' no party. An' you ain't usually gettin' no haircut on'a Wednesday neither. Sumpin's up."

"You dreamin', man. Party gonna be Saturday night an' you welcome t'come."

"'Uh-huh." He eyed me warily. "Whas all this got to do with Frank?"

My stomach filled with ice water but I didn't let it show. "This ain't got nuthin' t'do with Frank Green, man. I just want some liquor."

"Alright. Sounds good. You know I be around if they's a party t'be had."

"See ya then," I said. I was hoping that I'd still be alive.

All I had to do was live for twenty-four hours, until Frank made his weekly rounds.

I stopped by Joppy's on the way back from the liquor store.

It felt like home to see him buffing that marble top. But I was uncomfortable. I had always respected Joppy as a friend. I was also a little wary of him because you had to be careful around a fighter.

When I got to the bar I dug both hands into the pockets of my cotton jacket. I had so much to say that, for a moment, I couldn't say anything.

"What you starin' at, Ease?"

"I don't know, Jop."

Joppy laughed and ran his hand over his bald head. "What you mean?"

"That girl called me the other night."

"What girl is that?"

"The one your friend's lookin' for."

"Uh-huh." Joppy put down his rag and placed his hands on the bar. "That's pretty lucky, I guess."

"I guess so."

The bar was empty. Joppy and I were studying each other's eyes.

"But I don't think it was luck, really," I said.

"No?"

"No, Joppy, it was you."

The muscles in Joppy's forearms writhed when he clenched his fists. "How you figure?"

"It's the only answer, Jop. You and Coretta were the only ones who knew I was lookin' for her. I mean DeWitt Albright knew but he'd'a just gone after the girl if he knew where she was. And Coretta was still lookin' to get money from me, so she wouldn't want me knowin' she talked to Daphne. It was you, man."

"She could'a looked you up in the phone book."

"I ain't in the book, Joppy."

I didn't know for sure if I was right. Daphne could have found me some other way, but I didn't think so.

"Why, man?" I asked.

Joppy's hard face never let you know what he was thinking. But I don't think he suspected the lead pipes I had clenched in my pockets either.

After a long minute he gave me a friendly smile and said, "Don't get all hot, man. It ain't so bad."

"What you mean, ain't so bad?" I yelled. "Coretta's dead, your friend Albright is on my ass, the cops already brought me down once—"

"I din't mean for none'a that t'happen, Easy, you gotta believe it."

"Now Albright got me chasin' Frank Green," I blurted out.

"Frank Green?" Joppy's eyes tightened to birds' eyes.

"Yeah. Frank Green."

"Okay, Easy. Lemme tell ya how it is. Albright come here look-in' for that girl. He showed me the picture and right away I knew who it was . . ."

"How'd you know that?" I asked.

"Sometimes Frank bring her along when he deliverin' liquor. I figured she was his girl or sumpin'."

"But you didn't say nuthin' to Albright?"

"Naw. Frank's my supply, I ain't gonna get in bad with him. I just waited until he come back with her and I let her know, on the sly, that I got some information that she want to know. She called me and I give it to her."

"Why? Why you want to help her?"

Joppy flashed a smile at me that was as close to shy as he was likely to get. "She's a pretty girl, Easy. Very pretty. I wouldn't mind her bein' my friend."

"Why not just tell Frank?"

"And have him come in here swingin' that knife? Shit. Frank is crazy."

Joppy relaxed a little when he saw that I was listening. He picked up his rag again. "Yeah, Ease, I thought I could get you some money and send Albright on a wrong trail. It would'a all been fine if you had listened t'me and laid off lookin'."

"Why you had her call me?"

Joppy clamped his jaw so that the bones stood out under his ears. "She called me and wanted me to help her go somewhere, to some friend she said. But I didn't want none of it. You know I could help as long as all I had to do was from behind the bar, but I wasn't goin' nowhere."

"But why me?"

"I told her t'call ya. She wanna know what DeWitt want, and you the one workin' fo' him." Joppy hunched his shoulders. "I give her your number. I couldn't see where it hurt."

"So you just playin' me for the fool and then, when you fin-ished, you gimme t'her."

"Nobody made you take that man's money. Nobody made you see that girl."

He was right about that. He talked me into it, but I was hungry for that money too.

"Her friend was dead," I said.

"White guy?"

"Uh-huh. And Coretta James is dead, and whoever killed her also got to Howard Green."

"That's what I heard." Joppy threw the rag under the counter and brought out a short glass. While pouring my whiskey he said, "I din't mean fo' all this, Easy. Just tryin' t'help you and that girl."

"That girl is the devil, man," I said. "She got evil in every pocket."

"Maybe you should get out of it, Ease. Take a trip back east or down south or sumpin'."

"That's what Odell told me. But I ain't gonna run, man."

I knew what I had to do. I had to find Frank and tell him about the money that Carter offered. Frank was a businessman at heart. And if DeWitt Albright stood in the way of Frank's business I'd just stand to the side and let them fight it out.

Joppy filled my glass again. It was a kind of peace offering. He really hadn't tried to hurt me. It was just the lie that stuck in my craw.

"Whyn't you tell me 'bout the girl?" I asked him.

"I don't know, Easy. She wanted me t'keep it quiet like and"— Joppy's face softened—"I wanted to keep her . . . secret. To myself, ya know?"

I took my drink and offered Joppy a cigarette. We smoked our peace and sat in friendship. We didn't speak again for a long time.

Later on Joppy asked, "Who you think been killin' all them folks?"

"I don't know, man. Odell told me that the cops think it might

be a maniac. And maybe it was with Coretta and Howard but I
know who killed that Richard McGee."

"Who?"

"I can't see where it helps either of us for me to tell you. Best
t'keep that to myself."


I was thinking these things as I walked through the gate and up
the path to my house. It wasn't until I was almost to the door that
I realized that the gate wasn't double-latched, the way the post-
man usually left it.

Before I turned back to look an explosion went off in my head. I
started a long fall through the twilight toward the cement stair of
my front porch. But for some reason I didn't hit the stair. The
door flung open and I found myself face down on the couch. I
wanted to get up but the loud noise in my head made me dizzy.

Then he turned me over.

He was wearing a dark blue suit, so dark that you might have
mistaken it for black. He wore a black shirt. His black shoe was on
the cushion next to my head. There was a short-rimmed black
Stetson on his head. His face was as black as the rest of him. The
only color to Frank Green was his banana-colored tie, loosely
knotted at his throat.

"Hi, Frank." The words shot pain through my head.

Frank's right fist made a snickering sound and a four-inch
blade appeared, like a chrome-colored flame.

"Hear you been lookin' fo' me, Easy."

I tried to sit up but he shoved my face back down onto the
couch. "Hear you been lookin' fo' me," he said again.

"That's right, Frank. I need to talk to you. I gotta deal for you,
make us both five hundred dollars."

Frank's black face cracked into a white grin. He put his knee
against my chest and pressed the tip of his knife, just barely, into
my throat. I could feel the flesh prick and the blood trickle.

"I'm'a have t'kill you, Easy."

My first reaction was to look around to see if there was something that might save me but there was nothing except walls and furniture. Then I noticed something strange. The straight-back wood chair that I kept in the kitchen was pulled up to my sofa chair as if someone had used it for a footrest. I don't know why I concentrated on that; for all I knew Frank had pulled it out while I was still out of it.

"Hear me out," I said.

"What?"

"I might could make it seven-fifty."

"How a mechanic gonna get that kinda money?"

"Man wanna talk to a girl you know. Rich man. He pay that much just to talk."

"What girl?" Frank's voice was almost a growl.

"White girl. Daphne Monet."

"You a dead man, Easy," Frank said.

"Frank, listen to me. You got me wrong, man."

"You been nosin' all 'round after me. I been hearin' it. You even goin' where I'm doin' business and where I be drinkin'. I come back from my little business trip and now Daphne's gone and you in every hole I shit in." His hard yellow eyes were staring right into mine. "The cops lookin' fo' me too, Easy. Somebody kilt Coretta and I hear you was around 'fore she died."

"Frank . . ."

He pressed the blade a little harder. "You dead, Easy," he said and then he shifted the weight of his shoulder.

The voice said, "Don't cry or beg, Easy. Don't give this nigger the satisfaction."

"Evenin', Frank," somebody said in a friendly tone. It wasn't me. I could tell that it was real because Frank froze. He was still staring at me but his attention was at his back.

"Who's that?" he croaked.

"Been a long time, Frank. Must be ten years."

"That you, Mouse?"

"You got a good mem'ry, Frank. I always like a man got a good memory, cause nine times outta eleven he's a smart man could 'preciate a tough problem. 'Cause you know I got a problem here, Frank."

"What's that?"

Right then the phone rang, and I'll be damned if Mouse didn't answer it!

"Yeah?" he said. "Yeah, yeah, Easy's here but he kinda busy right now. Uh-huh, yeah, sure. Could he call you right back? No? Okay. Yeah. Yeah, try back in 'bout a hour, he be free by then."

I heard him put the phone back on the hook. I couldn't see past Frank Green's chest.

"Where was I . . . oh yeah, I was gonna tell ya my problem. You see, Frank, I got this here long-barreled forty-one-caliber pistol pointed at the back'a yo' head. But I cain't shoot it 'cause I'm afraid that if you fall you gonna cut my partner's throat. Thas some problem, huh?"

Frank just stared at me.

"So what you think I should do, Frank? I know you just itchin' t'cut on poor Easy but I don't think you gonna live t'smile 'bout it, brother."

"Ain't none'a yo' business, Mouse."

"I tell you what, Frank. You put down that knife right there on the couch an' I let you live. You don't an' you dead. I ain't gonna count or no bullshit like that now. Just one minute and I'm'a shoot."

Frank slowly took the knife from my throat and placed it on the couch, where it could be seen from behind.

"Okay now, stand away and sit over in this here chair."

Frank did as he was told and there was Mouse, beautiful as he could be. His smile glittered. Some of the teeth were rimmed with gold and some were capped. One tooth had a gold rim with a blue jewel in it. He wore a plaid zoot suit with Broadway suspenders

down the front of his shirt. He had spats on over his patent
leather shoes and the biggest pistol I had ever seen held loosely
in his left hand.

Frank was staring at that pistol too.

Knifehand was a bad man but there wasn't a man in his right
mind who knew Mouse who didn't give him respect.

"'S'appenin', Easy?"

"Mouse," I said. Blood covered the front of my shirt; my hands
were shaking.

"Want me t'kill'im, Ease?"

"Hey!" Frank yelled. "We hadda deal!"

"Easy my oldest partner, man. I shoot yo' ugly face off and ain't
nuthin' you gonna say t'stop me."

"We don't need t'kill'im. All I need is a couple of answers." I
realized that I didn't need Frank if I had Mouse on my side.

"Then get t'askin', man," Mouse grinned.

"Where's Daphne Monet?" I asked Green. He just stared at
me, his eyes sharp as his knife.

"You heard'im, Frank," Mouse said. "Where is she?"

Frank's eyes weren't so sharp when he looked at Mouse but he
stayed quiet anyway.

"This ain't no game, Frank." Mouse let the pistol hang down
until the muzzle was pointing at the floor. He walked up to Frank;
so close that Knifehand could have grabbed him. But Frank
stayed still. He knew that Mouse was just playing with him.

"Tell us what we wanna know, Frankie, or I'm'a shoot ya."

Frank's jaw set and his left eye half closed. I could see that
Daphne meant enough to him that he was ready to die to keep her
safe.

Mouse raised the pistol so that it was pointing to the soft place
under Frank's jaw.

"Let'im go," I said.

"But you said you had a five-hundred-dollar deal." Mouse was
hungry to hurt Frank, I could hear it in his tone.

"Let'im go, man. I don't want him killed in my house." I thought maybe Mouse would sympathize with keeping blood off the furniture.

"Gimme your keys then. I take him for a drive." Mouse smiled an evil grin. "He'll tell me what I wanna know."

Without warning Mouse pistol-whipped Frank three times; every blow made a sickening thud. Frank fell to his knees with the dark blood coming down over his dark clothes.

When Frank fell to the floor I jumped between him and Mouse.

"Let'im go!" I cried.

"Get outta my way, Easy!" There was bloodlust in Mouse's voice.

I grabbed for his arm. "Let him be, Raymond!"

Before anything else could happen I felt Frank pushing me from behind. I was propelled onto Mouse and we fell to the floor. I hugged Mouse to break my fall but also to keep him from shooting Frank. By the time the wiry little man got out from under me Frank had bolted out the door.

"Dammit, Easy!" He turned with the pistol loosely aimed at me. "Don't you never grab me when I got a gun in my hand! You crazy?"

Mouse ran to the window but Frank was gone.

I hung back for a moment while Mouse calmed down.

After a minute or two he turned away from the window and looked down at his jacket, "Look at the blood you got on my coat, Easy! Why you wanna go and do that?"

"I need Frank Green alive. You kill him and one of my sources dries up."

"What? What that got to do with this mess?" Mouse took off his jacket and draped it over his arm. "That the bathroom?" he asked, pointing to the door.

"Yeah," I said.

He hung the pistol in his belt and carried the stained jacket to the toilet. I heard the water running.

When Mouse returned I was staring out the front window, through the slatted blinds.

"He ain't gonna be back t'night, Easy. Tough man like Frank seen too much death to want it on him."

"What you doin' here, Mouse?"

"Din't you call Etta?"

"Yeah?"

Mouse was looking at me, shaking his head and smiling.

"Easy, you changed."

"How's that?"

"You use' t'be kinda scared of everything. Take them little nigger jobs like gardenin' and cleanin' up. Now you got this nice house and you fuckin' some white man's girl."

"I ain't touched her, man."

"Not yet."

"Not ever!"

"Com'on Easy, this is the Mouse you talkin' to. A woman look twice at you an' you cain't say no. I should know."

I had messed around with Etta behind Mouse's back when they were just engaged. He found out about it but he didn't care. Mouse never worried about what his women did. But if I'd touched his money he'd have killed me straight away.

"So what you doin' here?" I asked to change the subject.

"First thing I want to figure is how I can get that money you told Frank about."

"No, Mouse. That has nuthin' t'do with you."

"You gotta man comin' here wanna kill you, Easy. Yo' eye look like hamburger. Man, I could see why you called me, you could use some help."

"No, Raymond, I did call ya, but that was when I was low. I mean I'm glad you saved me, man, but your kinda help ain't nuthin' I could use."

"Com'on Easy, you let me in on it an' we both come outta this wit' sumpin'."

He had said almost exactly the same words to me eight years before. When everything was over I had two dead men on my soul.

"No, Raymond."

Mouse stared at me for a minute. He had light gray eyes; eyes that seemed to see through everything.

"I said no, Mouse."

"Tell me 'bout it, Easy." He leaned back into his chair. "Ain't no other way, brother."

"What you mean?"

"Nigger cain't pull his way out the swamp wit'out no help, Easy. You wanna hole on t'this house and git some money and have you some white girls callin' on the phone? Alright. That's alright. But, Easy, you gotta have somebody at yo' back, man. That's just a lie them white men give 'bout makin' it on they own. They always got they backs covered."

"All I want is my chance," I said.

"Yeah, Easy. Yeah, that's all."

"But let me tell ya," I said. "I'm scared t'get mixed up wit' you, man."

Mouse flashed his golden smile at me. "What?"

"You remember when we went to Pariah? To get yo' weddin' money?"

"Yeah?"

"DaddyReese an' Clifton died, Ray. They died 'cause'a you."

When Mouse stopped smiling the light in the room seemed to go dim. All of a sudden he was pure business; he'd just been playing with Frank Green.

"What you mean?"

"You kilt'em, man! You, an' me too! Clifton came to me two nights fo' he died. He wanted me t'tell'im what t'do. He tole me how you planned t'use him." I felt the tears pressing my eyes but held them back. "But I didn't say nuthin'. I just let that boy go.

Now ev'rybody think he killed Reese but I know it was you. And that hurts me, man."

Mouse rubbed his mouth, never even blinking.

"That been botherin' you all this time?" He sounded surprised.

"Yeah."

"That was a lotta years ago, Easy, an' you wasn't even there, really."

"Guilt don't tell time," I said.

"Guilt?" He said the words as if it had no meaning. "You mean like what *I* did makes you feel bad?"

"That's right."

"I tell you what then," he said, putting his hands up at his shoulders. "You let me work on this with you and I let you run the show."

"Whas that mean?"

"I ain't gonna do nuthin' you don't tell me t'do."

"Everything I say?"

"Whatever you say, Easy. Maybe you gonna show me how a poor man can live wit'out blood."

We didn't touch the whiskey.

I told Mouse what I knew; it wasn't much. I told him that De-Witt Albright was up to no good. I told him that I could get a thousand dollars for information about Daphne Monet because there was a price on her head.

When he asked me what she had done I looked him in the eye and said, "I don't know."

Mouse puffed on a cigarette while he listened to me. "Frank come back here an' you might not get out again," he said when I stopped talking.

"We ain't gonna be here neither, man. We both leave in the

morning an' follow this thing down." I told him where he could find DeWitt Albright. I also told him how he could get in touch with Odell Jones and Joppy if he needed help. The plan was to put Mouse on Frank's trail and I'd look into the places I had seen Daphne. We'd come up with the girl and improvise from there.

It felt good to be fighting back. Mouse was a good soldier, though I worried about him following orders. And if I had the whole thing scammed out right we'd both come out on top; I'd still be alive and have my house too.

Mouse fell asleep on my living room sofa. He was always a good sleeper. He once told me that they'd have to wake him for his execution because "the Mouse ain't gonna miss his rest."

didn't tell Mouse everything.

I didn't tell him about the money Daphne stole or the rich white man's name; or that I knew his name. Mouse probably meant to keep his word to me; he could keep from killing if he tried. But if he got a whiff of that thirty thousand dollars I knew that nothing would hold him back. He would have killed *me* for that much money.

"All you have to do is worry about Frank," I told him. "Just find out where he goes. If he leads you to the girl then we got it made. Understand me, Raymond, I just wanna find the girl, there ain't no reason to hurt Frank."

Mouse smiled at me. "Don't worry, Ease. I was just mad when I seen'im over you like that. You know, it made me kinda wanna teach him a lesson."

"You gotta watch him," I said. "He know how to use that knife."

"Shit!" Mouse spat. "I'as born wit' a knife in my teefs."

The police met us as we were leaving the house at eight in the morning.

"Shit."

"Mr. Rawlins," Miller said. "We came to ask you a few more questions."

Mason was grinning.

"Guess I better be goin', Easy," Mouse said.

Mason put a fat hand against Mouse's chest. "Who are you?" he asked.

"Name is Navrochet," Mouse said. "I just come by t'get some money he owe me."

"Money for what?"

"Money I lent him over a year ago." Mouse produced a wad of bills, the topmost of which was a twenty.

The broad grin on Mason's fat face didn't make him any prettier. "And he's just got it now?"

"Better have," Mouse said. "Or you officers would be comin' fo' me."

The cops exchanged meaningful glances.

"Where do you live, Mr. Navrochet?" Miller asked. He took out a pad and a pen.

"Twenty-seven thirty-two and a half, down on Florence. It's upstairs in the back," Mouse lied.

"We might have some questions for you later," Miller informed him as he wrote down the address. "So you should stick around town."

"Anything you boys want. I work at that big World Carwash on Crenshaw. You know I be there if I ain't at my house. See ya, Easy." Mouse went swinging his arms and whistling. I never did figure out how he knew the streets so well to lie like that.

"Shall we go in?" Miller gestured back toward the house.

They put me in a chair and then they stood over me, like they meant business.

"What do you know about this Richard McGee?" Miller asked me.

When I looked up I saw them searching my face for the truth.

"Who?" I said.

"You heard me," Miller said.

"I don't know who you said." I was stalling for time to figure out what they knew. Mason laid a heavy hand on my shoulder.

"LAPD found a dead man in his house in Laurel Canyon last night," Miller told me. "Richard McGee. He had a hand-written note on his table."

Miller held out the scrap of paper to me. On it was scrawled "C. James."

"Sound familiar?" Miller asked.

I tried to look stupid; it wasn't very difficult.

"How about Howard Green? You know him?" Miller put his foot on my table and leaned forward so far that his gaunt face was no more than a few inches from mine.

"No."

"You don't? He goes to that nigger bar you were at with Coretta James. That place just isn't big enough to hide in."

"Well, maybe I'd know his face if you showed me," I said.

"That would be kinda hard," Mason growled. "He's dead and his face looks like hamburger."

"What about Matthew Teran, Ezekiel?" Miller asked.

"'Course I know him. He was runnin' for mayor up till a few weeks ago. What the hell is this, anyway?" I stood up, faking disgust.

Miller said, "Teran called us the night we arrested you. He

wanted to know if we'd found out who killed his driver, Howard Green."

I gave him a blank stare.

"We told him no," Miller continued. "But there had been another murder, Coretta James' murder, that had the same kind of violence related to it. He was real interested, Easy. He wanted to know all about you. He even came down to the station and had us point you out to him and his new driver."

I remembered the peephole in the door.

"I ain't never even met the man," I said.

"No?" Miller said. "Teran's body was found in his downtown office this morning. He had a nice little bullet hole through his heart."

The spike through my head drove me back into the chair.

"We don't think you had anything to do with it, Ezekiel. At least, we can't prove anything. But you have to know something . . . and we have all day to ask you questions."

Mason grinned wide enough to show me his flaring red gums.

"I don't know what you guys are talking about. Maybe I know this dude Howard Green. I mean if he goes to John's I prob'ly know what he looks like but I don't know nuthin' else."

"I think you do, Ezekiel. And if you do but you don't tell us then things are going to get bad. Real bad for you."

"Man, I don't know a thing. People gettin' killed ain't gotta thing to do with me. You took me in. You know I ain't got no record. I had me a drink with Dupree and Coretta and that's all. You cain't hang me for that."

"I can if I prove that you were in McGee's house."

I noticed that Miller had a small crescent scar under his right eye. It seemed to me that I always knew he had that scar. Like I knew it and I didn't know it at the same time.

"I ain't been there," I said.

"Where?" Miller asked eagerly.

"I ain't been to no dead man's house."

"There's a big fat fingerprint on the knife, Ezekiel. If it's yours then you're fried."

Mason took my jacket from a chair and held it out to me, like a butler might. He thought he had me so he could afford being polite.

They took me back down to the station for fingerprinting, then they sent the prints downtown to be compared against the one found on the knife.

Miller and Mason took me to the little room again for another round of questions.

They kept asking the same things. Did I know Howard Green? Did I know Richard McGee? Miller kept threatening to go down to John's and find somebody who could tie me to Green but we both knew that he was throwing a bluff. Back in those days there wasn't one Negro in a hundred who'd talk to the police. And those that did were just as likely to lie as anything else. And John's crowd was an especially close one so I was safe, at least from the testimony of friends.

But I was worried about that fingerprint.

I knew that I hadn't touched the knife but I didn't know what the police were up to. If they really wanted to catch who did the killing then they'd be fair and check my prints against the knife's and let me go. But maybe they needed a culprit. Maybe they just wanted to close the books because their record hadn't been so good over the year. You never could tell when it came to the cops and a colored neighborhood. The police didn't care about crime among Negros. I mean, some soft-hearted cops got upset if a man killed his wife or did any such harm to a child. But the kind of violence that Frank Green dished out, the business kind of violence, didn't get anybody worried. The papers hardly ever even reported a colored murder. And when they did it was way in the back pages.

So if they wanted to get me for Howard Green's death, or Coretta's, then they might just frame me to cut down the paperwork. At least that's what I thought at the time.

The difference was that two white men had died also. To kill a white man was a real crime. My only hope was that these cops were interested in finding the real criminal.

I was still being questioned that afternoon when a young man in a loose brown suit entered the small room. He had a large brown envelope that he handed to Miller. He whispered something into Miller's ear and Miller nodded seriously as if he had heard something that was very important. The young man left and Miller turned to me; it was the only time I ever saw him smile.

"I got the answer on the fingerprints right here in this package, Ezekiel," he grinned.

"Then I guess I can go now."

"Uh-uh."

"What's it say?" Mason was frisking from side to side like a dog whose master had just come home.

"Looks like we got our killer."

My heart was beating so fast that I could hear the pulse in my ear. "Naw, man. I wasn't there."

I looked into Miller's face, not giving away an ounce of fear. I looked at him and I was thinking of every German I had ever killed. He couldn't scare me and he couldn't bring me down either.

Miller pulled out a white sheet from the envelope and looked at it. Then he looked at me. Then to the paper again.

"You can go, Mr. Rawlins," he said after a full minute. "But we're going to get you again. We're going to bring you down for something, Ezekiel, you can bank on that."

"Easy! Easy, over here!" Mouse hissed to me from my car across the street.

"Where'd you get my keys?" I asked him as I climbed in the passenger's side.

"Keys? Shit, man, all you gotta do is rub a couple'a sticks together an' you could start this thing."

The ignition had a bunch of taped wires hanging from it. Some other time I might have been mad but all I could do then was laugh.

"I was startin' t'think that I'd have t'come in after you, Ease," Mouse said. He patted the pistol that sat between us on the front seat.

"They don't have enough to hold me, yet. But if something don't happen fo' them real soon they might just take it in their heads to fo'get ev'rybody else an' drag me down."

"Well," Mouse said, "I found out where Dupree is holed up. We could go stay with him and figger what's next."

I wanted to talk to Dupree but there was something that was more important.

"We go over there a little later, but first I want you to drive somewhere."

"Where's that?"

"Go up here to the corner and take a left," I said.

**P**ortland Court was a horseshoe of tiny apartments not far from Joppy's place, near 107th and Central. There were sixteen little porches and doorways staggered in a semicircle around a small yard that had seven stunted magnolia trees growing in brick pots. It was early evening and the tenants, mostly old people, were sitting inside the screened doorways, eating their dinners off of portable aluminum stands. Radios played from every house. Mouse and I waved to folks and said hello as we made it back to number eight.

That door was closed.

I knocked on it and then I knocked again. After a few minutes we heard something crash and then heavy footsteps toward the door.

"Who's that?" an angry voice that might have had some fear in it called out.

"It's Easy!" I shouted.

The door opened and Junior Fornay stood there, in the gray haze of the screen door, wearing blue boxer shorts and a white tee-shirt.

"What you want?"

"I wanna talk about your call the other night, Junior. I gotta couple'a things I wanna ask."

I reached to pull the door open but Junior threw the latch from the inside.

"If you wanted t'talk you should'a done it then. Right now I gotta get some sleep."

"Why'ont you open the do', Junior, fo' I have t'shoot it down," Mouse said. He had been standing to the side of the door, where Junior couldn't see, but then he stood out in plain sight.

"Mouse," Junior said.

I wondered if he was still anxious to see my friend again.

"Open up, Junior, Easy an' me ain't got all night."

We went in and Junior smiled as if he wanted to make us feel at home.

"Wanna beer, boys? I gotta couple'a quarts in the box."

We got drinks and lit up cigarettes that Junior offered. He seated us on folding chairs he had placed around a card table.

"What you need?" he asked after a while.

I took a handkerchief from my pocket. It was the same handkerchief that I used to pick up something from the floor at Richard McGee's.

"Recognize this?" I asked Junior as I opened it on his table.

"What's a cigarette butt gotta do with me?"

"It's yours, Junior, Zapatas. You the only one I know cheap enough to smoke this shit. And you see how somebody just let it drop to the floor and burn so that the paper on the bottom is just charred but not ash?"

"So what? So what if it's mine?"

"I found this here on the floor of a dead man's house. Richard

McGee was his name. Somebody had just given him Coretta James' name; somebody who knew that Coretta was with that white girl."

"So what?" Like magic, sweat appeared on Junior's brow.

"Why'd you kill Richard McGee?"

"Huh?"

"Ain't no time to play, Junior. I know you the one killed him."

"Whas wrong wit' Easy, Mouse? Somebody hit him in the head?"

"This ain't no time to play, Junior. You killed him and I need to know why."

"You crazy, Easy. You crazy!"

Junior jumped up out of his chair and made like he was about to leave.

"Sit down, Junior," Mouse said.

Junior sat.

"Tell me what happened, Junior."

"I don't know what you talkin' 'bout, man. I don't even know who you mean."

"All right," I said, showing him my palms. "But if I go to the police they gonna find out that that fingerprint they got on the knife belong to you."

"What knife?" Junior's eyes looked like moons.

"Junior, you got to listen real close to this. I got troubles of my own right now and I ain't got the time to worry 'bout you. The night I was at John's that white man was there. Hattie had you carry him home and then he must'a paid you for Coretta's name. That's when you killed him."

"I ain't killed nobody."

"That fingerprint gonna prove you wrong, man."

"Shit!"

I knew I was right about Junior but that wasn't going to help me if he didn't want to talk. The problem was that Junior wasn't afraid of me. He was never afraid of any man that he felt he could best in a fight. Even though I had the information that would prove him guilty he didn't worry because I was his inferior in combat.

"Kill'im, Raymond," I said.

Mouse grinned and stood up. The pistol was just there, in his hand.

"Wait a minute, man. What kinda shit you tryin' t'pull here?" Junior said.

"You killed Richard McGee, Junior. And the next night you called me 'cause it had somethin' to do with that girl I was lookin' for. You wanted to find out what I knew but when I didn't tell you anything you hung up. But you killed him and you gonna tell me why or Mouse is gonna waste your ass."

Junior licked his lips and threw himself around in his chair like a child throwing a fit.

"What you wanna come messin' wit' me fo', man? What I do to you?"

"Tell it the way it happened, Junior. Tell me and maybe I forget what I know."

Junior threw himself around some more. Finally he said, "He was down at the bar the night you come in."

"Yeah?"

"Hattie didn't want him inside so she told him to go. But he must'a already been drunk 'cause he kinda like passed out on the street. So Hattie got me to go out an' check on'im 'cause she didn't want no trouble with him out there. So I go out to help him to his car, or whatever."

Junior stopped to take a drink of beer but then he just stared out the window.

"Get on with it, Junior," Mouse said at last. He wanted to move on.

"He say he give me twenty dollars for to know 'bout that girl you was askin' on, Easy. He said that he give me a hundred if I was to drive him home and tell'im how to find the white girl."

"I know you took that." Mouse was working a toothpick between his front teeth.

"Lotta money," Junior smiled hopefully at the warmth Mouse showed. "Yeah, I drove him home. And I told'im that I seen the girl he was lookin' for, with Coretta James. Just'a white girl anyway, why should I care?"

"Then why you kill'im?" I asked.

"He wanted me to give Frank Green a message. He says that he give me the money after I do that."

"Yeah?"

"I tole him that he could fuck dat! I did what he wanted and if he needed sumpin' else we could talk about that after I got paid." Junior got a wild look in his eye. "He told me I could walk home with my twenty if that's how I felt. Then he bad-mouth me some an' turn off into the other room. Shit! Fo' all I know'd he had a pistol in there. I got a knife from the sink an' goes in after'im. He could'a had a gun in there, ain't that right, Raymond?"

Mouse sipped his beer and stared at Junior.

"What he want you to say to Frank?" I asked.

"He want me t'tell'im that him an' his friends had sumpin' on the girl."

"Daphne?"

"Yeah," Junior said. "He say that they got sumpin' on'er and they should all talk."

"What else?"

"Nuthin'."

"You just killed him 'cause he might'a hadda gun?"

"You ain't got no cause to tell the cops, man," Junior said.

He was sunken in his chair, like an old man. He disgusted me. He was brave enough to take on a smaller man, he was brave enough to stab an unarmed drunk, but Junior couldn't stand up to answer for his crimes.

"He ain't worf livin'," the voice whispered in my head.

"Let's go," I said to Mouse.

Dupree was at his sister's house, out past Watts, in Compton. Bula had a night job as a nurse's assistant at Temple Hospital so it was Dupree who answered our knock.

"Easy," he said in a quiet voice. "Mouse."

"Pete!" Mouse was bright. "That pigtails I smell?"

"Yeah, Bula made some this mo'nin'. Black-eyes too."

"You don't need to show me, I just run after my nose."

Mouse went around Dupree toward the smell. We stood in the tiny entrance looking at each other's shoulders. I was still half outside. Two crickets sounded from the rose beds that Bula kept.

"I'm sorry 'bout Coretta, Pete. I'm sorry."

"All I wanna know is why, Easy. Why somebody wanna kill her like that?" When Dupree looked up at me I saw that both of his eyes were swollen and dark. I never asked but I knew that those bruises were part of his police interrogation.

"I don't know, man. I can't see why someone wanna do that t'anybody."

Tears were coming down Dupree's face. "I do it to the man done it to her." He looked me in the eye. "When I find out who it was, Easy, I'm'a kill that man. I don't care who he is."

"You boys better com'on in," Mouse said from the end of the hall. "Food's on the table."

Bula had rye in the cabinet. Mouse and Dupree drank it. Dupree had been crying and upset the whole evening. I asked him some questions but he didn't know anything. He told us about how the police had questioned him and held him for two days without telling him why. But when they finally told him about Coretta he broke down so they could see that it wasn't him.

Dupree drank steady while he told his story. He got more and more drunk until he finally passed out on the sofa.

"That Dupree is a good man," Mouse slurred. "But he jus' cain't hold his liquor."

"You got your sails pretty far up too, Raymond."

"You callin' me drunk?"

"All I'm sayin' is that you been puttin' it away along wit'im and you could be sure that you wouldn't pass no breath test neither."

"If I was drunk," he said, "could I do this?"

Mouse, moving as fast as I've ever seen a man move, reached into his fancy jacket and came out with that long-barreled pistol. The muzzle was just inches from my forehead.

"Ain't a man in Texas could outdraw me!"

"Put it down, Raymond," I said as calmly as I could.

"Go on," Mouse dared, as he put the pistol back in his shoulder holster. "Go fo' your gun. Les see who gets kilt."

My hands were on my knees. I knew that if I moved Mouse would kill me.

"I don't have a gun, Raymond. You know that."

"You fool enough to go without no piece then you must wanna be dead." His eyes were glazed and I was sure that he didn't see me. He saw somebody, though, some demon he carried around in his head.

He drew the pistol again. This time he cocked the hammer. "Say your prayers, nigger, 'cause I'm'a send you home."

"Let him go, Raymond," I said. "He done learned his lesson good enough. If you kill'im then he won't have got it." I was just talking.

"He fool enough t'call me out an' he ain't even got no gun! I kill the motherfucker!"

"Let him live, Ray, an' he be scared'a you whenever you walk in the room."

"Motherfucker better be scared. I kill the motherfucker. I kill'im!"

Mouse nodded and let the pistol fall down into his lap. His head fell to his chest and he was asleep; just like that!

I took the gun and put it on the table in the kitchen.

Mouse always kept two smaller pistols in his bag, I knew that from our younger days. I got one of them and left a note for Dupree and him. I told them that I had gone home and that I had Mouse's gun. I knew he wouldn't mind as long as I told him about it.

I drove down my block twice before I was sure no one was waiting for me in the streets. Then I parked around the corner so that anyone coming up to my place would think I was gone.

When I had the key in my lock the phone started ringing. It was on the seventh ring before I got to it.

"Easy?" She sounded as sweet as ever.

"Yeah, it's me. I thought you'd be halfway to New Orleans by now."

"I've been calling you all night. Where have you been?"

"Havin' fun. Makin' all kinds'a new friends. The police want me to come down there and live wit'em."

She took my joke about friends seriously. "Are you alone?"

"What do you want, Daphne?"

"I have to talk with you, Easy."

"Well go on, talk."

"No, no. I have to see you. I'm scared."

"I don't blame ya for that. I'm scared just talkin' to ya on the phone," I said. "But I need to talk to ya though. I need to know some things."

"Come meet me and I'll tell you everything you need to know."

"Okay. Where are you?"

"Are you alone? I only want you to know where I am."

"You mean you don't want your boyfriend Joppy to know where you hidin'?"

If she was surprised that I knew about Joppy she didn't show it.

"I don't want *anybody* to know where I am, but you. Not Joppy and not that other friend that you said was visiting."

"Mouse?"

"Nobody! Either you promise me or I hang up right now."

"Okay, okay fine. I just got in and Mouse ain't even here. Tell me where you are and I'll come get ya."

"You wouldn't lie to me, would you, Easy?"

"Naw. I just wanna talk, like you."

She gave me the address of a motel on the south side of L.A.

"Hurry up, Easy. I need you," she said before hanging up. She got off the phone so quickly that she didn't give me the number of her room.

I scribbled a note, making my plans as I wrote. I told Mouse that he could find me at a friend's house, Primo's. I wrote RAY-

MOND ALEXANDER in bold letters across the top of the note because the only words Mouse could read were his own two names. I hoped that Dupree came with Mouse to read him the note and show him the way to Primo's house.

Then I rushed out the door.

I found myself driving in the L.A. night again. The sky toward the valley was coral with skinny black clouds across it. I didn't know why I was going alone to get the girl in the blue dress. But for the first time in quite a while I was happy and expectant.

The Sunridge was a smallish pink motel, made up of two rectangular buildings that came together in an "L" around an asphalt parking lot. The neighborhood was mostly Mexican and the woman who sat at the manager's desk was a Mexican too. She was a full-blooded Mexican Indian; short and almond-eyed with deep olive skin that had lots of red in it. Her eyes were very dark and her hair was black, except for four strands of white which told me that she had to be older than she looked.

She stared at me, the question in her eyes.

"Lookin' for a friend," I said.

She squinted a little harder, showing me the thick webbing of wrinkles at the corners of her eyes.

"Monet is her last name, French girl."

"No men in the rooms."

"I just have to talk with her. We can go out for coffee if we can't talk here."

She looked away from me as if to say our talk was over.

"I don't mean to be disrespectful, ma'am, but this girl has my money and I'm willing to knock on every door until I find her."

She turned toward the back door but before she could call out I said, "Ma'am, I'm willing to fight your brothers and sons to talk to this woman. I don't mean her any harm, or you neither, but I have got to have words with her."

She sized me up, putting her nose in the air like a leery dog checking out the new mailman, then she measured the distance to the back door.

"Eleven, far end," she said at last.

I ran down to the far end of the building.

While I knocked on number eleven's door I kept looking over my shoulder.

She had on a gray terrycloth robe and a towel was wrapped into a bouffant on her head. Her eyes were green right then and when she saw me she smiled. All the trouble she had and all the trouble I might have brought with me and she just smiled like I was a friend who was coming over for a date.

"I thought you were the maid," she said.

"Uh-uh," I mumbled. She was more beautiful than ever in the low-slung robe. "We should get outta here."

She was looking past my shoulder. "We better talk to the manager first."

The short woman and two big-bellied Mexican men were coming our way. One of the men was swinging a nightstick. They stopped a foot from me; Daphne closed the door a little to hide herself.

"Is he bothering you, Miss?" the manager asked.

"Oh no, Mrs. Guitierra. Mr. Rawlins is a friend of mine. He's taking me to dinner." Daphne was amused.

"I don't want no men in the rooms," the woman said.

"I'm sure he won't mind waiting in the car, would you, Easy?"

"I guess not."

"Just let us finish talking, Mrs. Guitierra, and he'll be a good man and go wait in his car."

One of the men was looking at me as if he wanted to break my head with his stick. The other one was looking at Daphne; he wanted something too.

When they moved back toward the office, still staring at us, I said to Daphne, "Listen. You wanted me to come here alone and here I am. Now I need the same feeling, so I want you to come with me to a place I know."

"How do I know that you aren't going to take me to the man Carter hired?" Her eyes were laughing.

"Uh-uh. I don't want any piece of him . . . I talked to your boyfriend Carter."

That took the smile from her face.

"You did! When?"

"Two, three days ago. He wants ya back and Albright wants that thirty thousand."

"I'm not going back to him," she said, and I knew that it was true.

"We can talk about that some other time. Right now you've got to get away from here."

"Where?"

"I know a place. You've got to get away from the men looking for you and I do too. I'll put you someplace safe and then we can talk about what we can do."

"I can't leave L.A. Not before I talk to Frank. He should be back by now. I keep calling though, and he's not home."

"The police tied him into Coretta, he's probably lyin' low."

"I have to talk to Frank."

"Alright, but we've got to get away from here right now."

"Wait a second," she said. She went into the room for a moment. When she reappeared she handed me a piece of paper wrapped around a wad of cash. "Go pay my rent, Easy. That way they won't bother us when they see us moving my bags."

Landlords everywhere love their money. When I paid Daphne's bill the two men left and the little woman even managed to smile at me.

Daphne had three bags but none of them was the beat-up old suitcase that she carried the first night we met.

We drove a long way. I wanted far from Watts and Compton so we went to East L.A.; what they call El Barrio today. Back then it was just another Jewish neighborhood, recently taken over by the Mexicans.

We drove past hundreds of poor houses, sad palm trees, and thousands of children playing and hollering in the streets.

We finally came to a dilapidated old house that used to be a mansion. It had a great cement porch with a high green roof and two big picture windows on each of the three floors. Two of the windows had been broken out; they were papered with cardboard and stuffed with rags. There were three dogs and eight old cars scattered and lounging around the red clay yard under the branches of a sickly and failing oak tree. Six or seven small children were playing among the wrecks. Hammered into the oak was a small wooden sign that read "rooms."

A grizzled old man in overalls and a tee-shirt was sitting in an aluminum chair at the foot of the stairs.

"Howdy, Primo," I waved.

"Easy," he said back to me. "You get lost out here?"

"Naw, man. I just wanted a little privacy so I figured to give you a try."

Primo was a real Mexican, born and bred. That was back in 1948, before Mexicans and black people started hating each other. Back then, before ancestry had been discovered, a Mexican and a Negro considered themselves the same. That is to say, just another couple of unlucky stiffs left holding the short end of the stick.

I met Primo when I became a gardener for a while. We worked together, with a team of men, taking on the large jobs in Beverly Hills and Brentwood. We even took care of a couple of places downtown, off of Sixth.

Primo was a good guy and he liked to run with me and my friends. He told us that he'd bought that big house so that he could turn it into a hotel. He was always begging us to come out and rent a room from him or to tell our friends about him.

He stood up when I came up the path. He only came up to my chest. "How's that?" he asked.

"You got somethin' with some privacy?"

"I got a little house out back that you and the señorita can have." He bent down to look at Daphne in the car. She smiled nicely for him.

"How much?"

"Five dollars for a night."

"What?"

"It's a whole house, Easy. Made for love." He winked at me.

I could have argued him down and I would have done it for fun, but I had other things on my mind.

"Alright."

I gave him a ten-dollar bill and he showed us to the path that led around the big house to the house out back. He started to come with us but I stopped him.

"Primo, my man," I said. "I'll come on up tomorrow an' we do some damage to a fifth of tequila. Alright?"

He smiled and thumped my arm before he turned to leave. I wished that my life was still so simple that all I was after was a wild night with a white girl.

The first thing we saw was a mass of flowering bushes with honey-suckle, snapdragons, and passion fruit weaving through. A jagged, man-sized hole was hacked from the branches. Past that doorway was a small building like a coach house or the gardener's quarters on a big estate. Three sides of the house were glass doors from ceiling to floor. All the doors could open outward onto the cement patio that surrounded these three sides of the house, but they were all shut. The front door was wood, painted green.

Long white curtains were drawn over all the windows.

Inside, the house was just a big room with a fallen-down spring-bed on one side and a two-burner gas range on the other. There was a table with a toaster on it and four spindly chairs. There was a big stuffed sofa upholstered with a dark brown material that had giant yellow flowers stitched into it.

"It's just beautiful," Daphne exclaimed.

My face must've said that she was crazy because she blushed a little and added, "Well it could use some work but I think we could make something out of it."

"Maybe if we tore it down . . ."

Daphne laughed and that was very nice. As I said before, she was like a child and her childish pleasure touched me.

"It is beautiful," she said. "Maybe not rich but it's quiet and it's private. Nobody else could see us here."

I put her bags down next to the sofa.

"I gotta go out for a little while," I said. Once I had her in place I saw how to get things moving.

"Stay."

"I got to, Daphne. I got two bad men and the L.A. police on my trail."

"What bad men?" She sat at the edge of the bed and crossed her legs. She had put on a yellow sundress at the motel, and it showed off her tan shoulders.

"The man your friend hired and Frank Green, your other friend."

"What does Frankie have to do with you?"

I went up to her and she stood to meet me. I pulled my collar down and showed her my gashed throat, saying, "That's what *Frankie* done to Easy."

"Oh, honey!" She reached out gently for my neck.

Maybe it was just the touch of woman that got to me or maybe it was finally realizing all that had happened to me in the previous week; I don't know.

"Look at that! That's the cops!" I said, pointing at the bruise on my eye. "I been arrested twice, blamed for four murders, threatened by people I wished I never met, and . . ." I felt that my liver was going to come out between my teeth.

"Oh my poor man," she said as she took me by the arm and led me to the bathroom. She didn't let go of my arm while she turned on the water for the bath. She was right there with me, unbuttoning my shirt, letting down my pants.

I was sitting there, naked on the toilet seat, and watching her go through the mirror-doored medicine cabinet. I felt something deep down in me, something dark like jazz when it reminds you that death is waiting.

"Death," the saxophone rasps. But, really, I didn't care.

**26**

**D**aphne Monet, a woman who I didn't know at all personally, had me laid back in the deep porcelain tub while she carefully washed between my toes and then up my legs. I had an erection lying flat against my stomach and I was breathing slowly, like a small boy poised to catch a butterfly. Every once in a while she'd say, "Shh, honey, it's all right." And for some reason that caused me pain.

When she finished with my legs she washed my whole body with a rough hand towel and a bar of soap that had pumice in it.

I never felt drawn to a woman the way I was to Daphne Monet. Most beautiful women make me feel like I want to touch them, own them. But Daphne made me look inside myself. She'd whisper a sweet word and I was brought back to the first time

I felt love and loss. I was remembering my mother's death, back when I was only eight, by the time Daphne got to my belly. I held my breath as she lifted the erection to wash underneath it; she looked into my face, with eyes that had become blue over the water, and stroked my erection up and down, twice. She smiled when she finished and pressed it back down against my flesh.

I couldn't say a word.

She stepped back from the tub and shrugged off her yellow dress in one long stretch then tossed it in the water over me and pulled down her pants. She sat on the toilet and urinated so loud that it reminded me more of a man.

"Hand me the paper, Easy," she said.

The roll was at the foot of of the bathtub.

She stood over the tub, with her hips pressed outward, looking down on me. "If my pussy was like a man's thing it'd be as big as your head, Easy."

I stood out of the tub and let her hold me around the testicles. As we went into the bedroom she kept whispering obscene suggestions in my ear. The things she said made me ashamed. I never knew a man who talked as bold as Daphne Monet.

I never liked it when women talked like that. I felt it was masculine. But, beneath her bold language, Daphne seemed to be asking me for something. And all I wanted was to reach as far down in my soul as I could to find it.

We yelled and screamed and wrestled all night long. Once, when I had fallen asleep, I woke to find her rubbing an ice cube down my chest. Once, at about 3 A.M., she took me out to the cement patio behind the bushes and made love to me as I lay back against a rough tree.

When the sun came up she nestled against my side on the bed and asked, "Does it hurt, Easy?"

"What?"

"Your thing, does it hurt?"

"Yeah."

"Is it sore?"

"It's more like the blood vessels ache."

She grabbed my penis. "Does it hurt for you to love me, Easy?"

"Yeah."

Her grip tightened. "I love it when you hurt, Easy. For us."

"Me too," I said.

"Do you feel it?"

"Yeah, I feel it."

She released me. "I don't mean that. I mean this house. I mean us here, like we aren't who they want us to be."

"Who?"

"They don't have names. They're just the ones who won't let us be ourselves. They never want us to feel this good or close like this. That's why I wanted to get away with you."

"*I* came to you."

She put her hand out again. "But I called you, Easy; I'm the one who brought you to me."

When I look back on that night I feel confused. I could say that Daphne was crazy but that would mean that I was sane enough to say, and I wasn't. If she wanted me to hurt, I loved to hurt, and if she wanted me to bleed, I would have been happy to open a vein. Daphne was like a door that had been closed all my life; a door that all of sudden flung open and let me in. My heart and chest opened as wide as the sky for that woman.

But I can't say that she was crazy. Daphne was like the chameleon lizard. She changed for her man. If he was a mild white man who was afraid to complain to the waiter she'd pull his head to her bosom and pat him. If he was a poor black man who had soaked up pain and rage for a lifetime she washed his wounds with a rough rag and licked the blood till it staunched.

It was mid-afternoon when I gave out. We had spent every moment in each other's arms. I didn't think about the police or Mouse or even DeWitt Albright. All I cared about was the pain I felt loving that white girl. But finally I pulled away from her and said, "We gotta talk, Daphne."

Maybe I was imagining it but her eyes flashed green for the first time since the bath.

"Well, what?" She sat up in the bed covering herself. I knew that I was losing her, but I was too satisfied to care.

"There's a lot of dead people, Daphne, and the police want me behind that. There's that thirty thousand dollars you stole from Mr. Carter and DeWitt Albright is on my ass for that."

"Any money I have is between me and Todd and I don't have anything to do with dead people or that Albright man. Nothing at all."

"Maybe you don't think so but Albright has the talent to make your business his . . ."

"So, what do you want from me?"

"Why'd Howard Green get killed?"

She stared through me as if I were a mirage. "Who?"

"Come on."

She looked away for a moment and then sighed. "Howard worked for a rich man named Matthew Teran. He was Teran's driver, chauffeur. Teran wanted to run for mayor but in that crowd you have to ask permission like. Todd didn't want Teran to do it."

"How come?" I asked.

"A while ago I met him, Teran I mean, and he was buying a little Mexican boy from Richard."

"The man we found?"

She nodded.

"And who was he?"

"Richard and I were"—she hesitated for a moment—"friends."

"Boyfriend?"

She nodded slightly. "Before I met Todd we spent some time together."

"The night I first started lookin' for you I ran into Richard in front of John's speak. Was he lookin' for you?"

"He might have been. He didn't want to let me go so he got together with Teran and Howard Green, to cause me trouble so they could get at Todd."

"What kind of trouble?" I asked.

"Howard knew something. Something about me."

"What?"

But she wouldn't answer that question.

"Who killed Howard?" I asked.

She didn't answer at first. She just played with the blankets, letting them fall down below her breasts.

"Joppy did," she said at last. She wouldn't meet my eye.

"Joppy!" I cried. "Why'd he want to do somethin' like that?" But I knew it was the truth even before I asked the question. It would take the kind of violence Joppy had to beat someone to death.

"Coretta too?"

Daphne nodded. The sight of her nakedness nauseated me right then.

"Why?"

"Sometimes I would go to Joppy's place with Frank. Just because Frank liked people to see me with him. And the last time I went there Joppy whispered that someone had been asking for me and that I should call him later to find out who. That's when I found out about that Albright man."

"But what about Howard and Coretta? What about them?"

"Howard Green had already come to me and told me that if I didn't do what he and his boss said they would ruin me. I told Joppy that I could get him a thousand dollars if he could make sure that Albright didn't find me and if he could talk with Howard."

"So he killed Howard?"

"It was a mistake, I think. Howard had a fast tongue. Joppy just got mad."

"But what about Coretta?"

"When she came to me I told Joppy about it. I told him that you were asking questions and"—she hesitated—"he killed her. He was scared by then. He'd already killed one man."

"Why didn't he kill you?"

She raised her head and threw her hair back. "I hadn't given him the money yet. He still wanted the thousand dollars. Anyway, he thought I was Frank's girl. Most people respect Frank."

"What's Frank to you?"

"Not anything you'd ever understand, Easy."

"Well, do you think he knows who killed Matthew Teran?"

"I don't know, Easy. I haven't killed anybody."

"Where's the money?"

"Somewhere. Not here. Not where you can get it."

"That money's gonna get you killed, girl."

"You kill me, Easy." She reached over to touch my knee.

I stood up. "Daphne, I gotta talk to Mr. Carter."

"I won't go back to him. Not ever."

"He just wants to talk. You don't have to be in love with him to talk."

"You don't understand. I do love him and because of that I can't ever see him." There were tears in her eyes.

"You makin' this hard, Daphne."

She reached for me again.

"Cut it out!"

"How much will Todd give you for me?"

"Thousand."

"Get me to Frank and I'll give you two."

"Frank tried to kill me."

"He won't do anything to you if I'm there."

"Take more than your smile to stop Frank."

"Take me to him, Easy; it's the only way you'll get paid."

"What about Mr. Carter and Albright?"

"They want me, Easy. Let Frank and me take care of it."

"What's Frank to you?" I asked again.

She smiled at me then. Her eyes turned blue and she laid back against the wall behind the bed. "Will you help me?"

"I don't know. I gotta get outta here."

"Why?"

"It's just too much," I said, remembering Sophie. "I need some air to breathe."

"We could stay here, honey; this is the only place for us."

"You wrong, Daphne. We don't have to listen to them. If we love each other then we can be together. Ain't no one can stop that."

She smiled, sadly. "You don't understand."

"You mean all you want from me is a roll in the hay. Get a little nigger-love out back and then straighten your clothes and put on your lipstick like you didn't ever even feel it."

She put out her hand to touch me but I moved away. "Easy," she said. "You have it wrong."

"Let's go get somethin' to eat," I said, looking away. "There's a Chinese place a few blocks from here. We could walk there through a shortcut out back."

"It'll be gone when we get back," she said.

I imagined that she had said that to lots of men. And lots of men would have stayed rather than lose her.

We dressed in silence.

When we were ready to go a thought came to me.

"Daphne?"

"Yes, Easy?" Her voice was bored.

"I wanted to know somethin'."

"What's that?"

"Why'd you call me yesterday?"

She turned green eyes on me. "I love you, Easy. I knew it from the first moment we met."

**C**how's Chow was a kind of Chinese diner that was common in L.A. back in the forties and fifties. There were no tables, just one long counter with twelve stools. Mr. Ling stood behind the counter in front of a long black stove on which he prepared three dishes: fried rice, egg foo young, and chow mein. You could have any one of these dishes with chicken, pork, shrimp, beef, or, on Sunday, lobster.

Mr. Ling was a short man who always wore thin white pants and a white tee-shirt. He had the tattoo of a snake that coiled out from under the left side of his collar, went around the back of his neck, and ended up in the middle of his right cheek. The snake's head had two great fangs and a long, rippling red tongue.

"What you want?" he yelled at me. I had been in Mr. Ling's

diner at least a dozen times but he never recognized me. He never recognized any customer.

"Fried rice," Daphne said in a soft voice.

"What kind?" Mr. Ling shouted. And then, before she could answer, "Pork, chicken, shrimp, beef!"

"I'll have chicken and shrimp, please."

"Cost more!"

"That'll be alright, sir."

I had egg foo young with pork.

Daphne seemed a little calmer. I had the feeling that if I could get her to open up, to talk to me, then I could talk some sense into her. I didn't want to force her to see Carter. If I forced her I could have been arrested for kidnapping and there was no telling how Carter would have reacted to her being manhandled. And maybe I loved her a little bit right then. She looked very nice in that blue dress.

"You know, I don't want to force anything on you, Daphne. I mean, the way I feel you don't ever have to kiss Carter again and it's okay with me."

I could feel her smile in my chest and in other parts of my body.

"You ever go to the zoo, Easy?"

"No."

"Really?" She was astonished.

"No reason t'see animals in cages far as I can see. They cain't help me and I cain't do nuthin' fo' them neither."

"But you can learn from them, Easy. The zoo animals can teach you."

"Teach what?"

She sat back and looked into the smoke and steam raised by Mr. Ling's stove. She was looking back into a dream.

"The first time my father took me to the zoo, it was in New Orleans. I was born in New Orleans." As she spoke she developed a light drawl. "We went to the monkey house and I remember thinking it smelled like death in there. A spider monkey was swinging from the nets that hung from the top of his cage; back and forth. Anyone with eyes could see that he was crazy from all those years of being locked away; but the children and adults were nudging each other and sniggering at the poor thing.

"I felt just like that ape. Swinging wildly from one wall to another; pretending I had somewhere to go. But I was trapped in my life just like that monkey. I cried and my father took me out of there. He thought that I was just sensitive to that poor creature. But I didn't care about a stupid animal.

"From then on we only went to the cages where the animals were more free. We watched the birds mainly. Herons and cranes and pelicans and peacocks. The birds were all I was interested in. They were so beautiful in their fine plumes and feathers. The male peacocks would spread out their tail feathers and rattle them at the hens when they wanted to mate. My daddy lied and said that they were just playing a game. But I secretly knew what they were doing.

"Then, at almost closing time, we passed the zebras. No one was around and Daddy was holding my hand. Two zebras were running back and forth. One was trying to avoid the other but the bully had cut off every escape. I yelled for my daddy to stop them because I worried that they were going to fight."

Daphne had grabbed on to my hand, she was so excited. I found myself worried; but I couldn't really tell what bothered me.

"They were right there next to us," she said. "At the fence, when the male mounted the female. His long, leathery thing jabbing in and out of her. Twice he came out of her completely, and spurted jissum down her flank.

"My daddy and I were holding hands so tight that it hurt me but I didn't say anything about it. And when we got back to the car he kissed me. It was just on the cheek at first but then he kissed me on the lips, like lovers do." Daphne had a faraway smile on her face. "But when he finished kissing me he started to cry. He put his head in my lap and I had to stroke his head for a long time and tell him that it was just fine before he'd even look up at me again."

The disgust must've shown on my face because she said, "You think that it was sick, what we did. But my daddy loved me. From then on, my whole fourteenth year, he'd take me to the zoo and the park. Always at first he'd kiss me like a father and his little girl but then we'd get alone someplace and act like real lovers. And always, always after he'd cry so sweet and beg me to forgive him. He bought me presents and gave me money, but I'd've loved him anyway."

I wanted to run away from her but I was too deep in trouble to act on my feelings so I tried to change the subject. "What's all that got to do with you goin' t'see Carter?" I asked.

"My daddy never took me anywhere again after that year. He left Momma and me in the spring and I never saw him again. Nobody ever knew about him and me and what had happened. But I knew. I knew that that was why he left. He just loved me so much that day at the zoo and he knew me, the real me, and whenever you know somebody that well you just have to leave."

"Why's that?" I wanted to know. "Why you have t'leave someone just when you get close?"

"It's not just close, Easy. It's something more."

"And that's what you had with Carter?"

"He knows me better than any other man."

I hated Carter then. I wanted to know Daphne like he did. I wanted her, even if knowing her meant that I couldn't have her.


Daphne and I took the back path, through the bushes, to the little house. Everything was fine.

I opened the door for her. She hadn't had anything else to say after her story about the zoo. I don't know why but I didn't have anything else to say either. Maybe it was because I didn't believe her. I mean, I believed that she believed the story, or, at least, she wanted to believe it, but there was something wrong with the whole thing.

Somewhere between the foo young and the check I decided to cut my losses. Daphne was too deep for me. Somehow I'd call Carter and tell him where she was. I'd wash my hands of the whole mess. I'm just in it for the money, I kept thinking to myself.

I was so busy having those thoughts that I didn't think to check the room. What was there to worry about anyway? So when Daphne gasped I was surprised to see DeWitt Albright standing at the stove.

"Evening, Easy," he drawled.

I reached for the pistol in my belt but before I could get to it an explosion went off in my head. I remember the floor coming up to my face and then there was nothing for a while.

I was on a great battleship in the middle
of the largest fire fight in the history of
war. The cannons were red hot and the crew and I were loading
those shells. Airplanes strafed the deck with machine-gun fire
that stung my arms and chest but I kept on hefting shells to the
man in front of me. It was dusk or early dawn and I was ex-
hilarated by the power of war.

Then Mouse came up to me and pulled me from the line. He
said, "Easy! We gotta get outta here, man. Ain't no reason t'die in
no white man's war!"

"But I'm fighting for freedom!" I yelled back.

"They ain't gonna let you go, Easy. You win the one and they
have you back on the plantation 'fore Labor Day."

I believed him in an instant but before I could run a bomb
rocked the ship and we started to sink. I was pitched from the

deck into the cold cold sea. Water came into my mouth and nose and I tried to scream but I was underwater. Drowning.

When I came awake I was dripping from the bucket of water that Primo had dumped on me. Water was in my eyes and down my windpipe.

"What happened, amigo? You have a fight with your friends?"

"What friends?" I asked suspiciously. For all I knew at that minute it was Primo who suckered me.

"Joppy and the white man in the white suit."

"White man?" Primo helped me to a sitting position. I was on the ground right outside the door of our little house. My head started clearing.

"Yeah. You okay, Easy?"

"What about the white man? When did he and Joppy get here?"

"About two, three hours ago."

"Two, three hours?"

"Yeah. Joppy asked me where you were and when I told him he drove the car back around the house. Then they took off about a little bit after that."

"The girl with'em?"

"I don't see no girl."

I pulled myself up and went through the house, Primo at my heels.

No girl.

I went out back and looked around but she wasn't there either. Primo came up behind me. "You guys have a fight?"

"Not much'a one. Can I use your phone, man?"

"Yeah, sure. It's right inside."

I called Dupree's sister but she said that he and Mouse had left in the early morning. Without Mouse I didn't know what to do. So I went out to my car and drove toward Watts.

The night was fully black with no moon and thick clouds that hid the stars. Every block or so there'd be a street lamp overhead, shining in darkness, illuminating nothing.

"Get out of it, Easy!"

I didn't say anything.

"You gotta find that girl, man. You gotta make this shit right."

"Fuck you!"

"Uh-uh, Easy. That don't make you brave. Brave is findin' that white man an' yo' friend. Brave is not lettin' them pull this shit on you."

"So what can I do?"

"You got that gun, don't ya? You think them men's gonna beat bullets?"

"They armed too, both of'em."

"All you gotta do is make sure they don't see ya comin'. Just like in the war, man. Make believe you is the night."

"But how I even find'em t'sneak up on? What you want me t'do? Look in the phone book?"

"You know where Joppy live, right? Les go look. An' if he ain't there you know they gotta be with Albright."

Joppy's house was dark and his bar was padlocked from the outside. The night watchman on duty at Albright's building, a fat, florid-faced man, said that Albright had moved out.

So I made up my mind to call information for every town north of Santa Monica. I got lucky and found DeWitt Albright on my first try. He lived on Route 9, in the Malibu Hills.

drove past Santa Monica into Malibu and found Route 9. It was just a graded dirt road. There I found three mailboxes that read: Miller, Korn, Albright. I passed the first two houses and drove a full fifteen minutes before getting to Albright's marker. It was far enough out that any death cry would go unheard.

It was a simple, ranch-style house, not large. There were no outside lights except on the front porch so I couldn't make out the color. I wanted to know what color the house was. I wanted to know what made jets fly and how long sharks lived. There was a lot I wanted to know before I died.

I could hear loud male voices and the woman's pleading before I got to the window.

Over the sill I saw a large room with a darkwood floor and a high ceiling. Before the blazing hearth sat a large couch covered with something like bear skin. Daphne was on the couch, naked, and the men, DeWitt and Joppy, stood over her. Albright was wearing his linen suit but Joppy was stripped to the waist. His big gut looked obscene hanging over her like that and it took everything I had not to shoot him right then.

"You don't want any more of that now do you, honey?" Albright was saying. Daphne spat at him and he grabbed her by the throat. "If I don't get that money you better believe I'll get the satisfaction of killing you, girl!"

I like to think of myself as an intelligent man but sometimes I just run on feelings. When I saw that white man choking Daphne I eased the window open and crawled into the room. I was standing there, pistol in hand—but DeWitt sensed me before I could draw a bead on him. He swung around with the girl in front of him. When he saw me he threw her one way and he leaped behind the couch! I moved to shoot but then Joppy bolted for the back door. That distracted me, and in my one moment of indecision the window behind me shattered and a shot, like a cannon roar, rang out. As I dove for cover behind a sofa chair I saw that DeWitt Albright had drawn his pistol.

Two more shots ripped through the back of the fat chair. If I hadn't moved to the side, down low, he would have gotten me then.

I could hear Daphne crying but there was nothing I could do for her. My big fear was that Joppy would come around outside and get me from behind. So I moved into a corner, still hidden, I hoped, from Albright's sight and in a position to see Joppy if he stuck his head in the window.

"Easy?" DeWitt called.

I didn't say a word. Even the voice was silent.

We waited two or three long minutes. Joppy didn't appear at the window. That bothered me and I began to wonder what other way he might come. But just as I was looking around I heard a noise as if DeWitt had lurched up. There was a dull thud and the sofa chair came falling backwards. He'd heaved a lamp at the top of its high back. The lamp shattered and, even as I pulled off a shot where I expected him to be, I saw DeWitt rise up a few feet farther on; he had that pistol leveled at me.

I heard the shot, and something else, something that seemed almost impossible: DeWitt Albright grunted, "Wha?"

Then I saw Mouse! The smoking pistol in his hand!

He'd come into the room through the door Joppy had taken.

More shots exploded. Daphne screamed. I jumped to cover her with my body. Splinters of wood jumped from the wall and I saw Albright hurl himself through a window at the other side of the room.

Mouse took aim but his gun wouldn't fire. He cursed, threw it down, and got a snub-nose from his pocket. He ran for the window but in that time I heard the Caddy's engine turn over; tires were slithering in the dirt before Mouse could empty his second chamber.

"DAMN!!" Mouse yelled. "DAMN DAMN DAMN!!!"

A cold draft, sucked in through the shattered window, washed over Daphne and me.

"I hit him, Easy!" He was grinning down on me with all those golden teeth.

"Mouse," was all I could say.

"Ain't ya glad t'see me, Ease?"

I got up and took the little man in my arms. I hugged him like I would hug a woman.

"Mouse," I said again.

"Com'on man, we gotta get yo' boy back here." He jerked his head toward the door he'd come through.

Joppy was on the floor in the kitchen. His arms and legs were behind him, hog-tied by an extension cord. There was thick blood coming from the top of his bald head.

"Les get him to the other room," Mouse said.

We got him to the chair and Mouse strapped him down.

Daphne wrapped herself in a blanket and shied to the end of the couch. She looked like a frightened kitten on her first Fourth of July.

All of a sudden Joppy's eyes shot open and he shouted, "Cut me aloose, man!"

Mouse just smiled.

Joppy was sweating, bleeding, and staring at us. Daphne was staring at the floor.

"Lemme go," Joppy whimpered.

"Shut up, man," Mouse said and Joppy quieted down.

"Can I have my clothes now?" Daphne's voice was thick.

"Sure, honey," Mouse said. "Right after we take care on some business."

"What's that?" I asked.

Mouse leaned forward to put his hand on my knee. It felt good to be alive and to be able to feel another man's touch. "I think you an' me deserve a little sumpin' fo' all this mess, don't you, Easy?"

"I give you half of everything I made, Ray."

"Naw, man," he said. "I don't want your money. I wanna piece'a that big pie Ruby over here sittin' on."

I didn't know why he called her Ruby, but I let it pass.

"Man, that's stolen money."

"That's the sweetest kind, Easy." He turned to her and smiled. "What about it, honey?"

"That's all Frank and I have. I won't give it up." I would have believed her if she wasn't talking to Mouse.

"Frank's dead." Mouse's face was completely deadpan.

Daphne looked at him for a moment and then she crumpled, just like a tissue, and started shaking.

Mouse went on, "Joppy the one did it, I figure. They found him beat to death in a alley just down from his bar."

When Daphne raised her head she had hate in her eyes, and

there was hate in her voice when she said, "Is that the truth, Raymond?" She was a different woman.

"Now am I gonna lie to you, Ruby? Your brother is dead."

I had only been in an earthquake once but the feeling was the same: The ground under me seemed to shift. I looked at her to see the truth. But it wasn't there. Her nose, cheeks, her skin color—they were white. Daphne was a white woman. Even her pubic hair was barely bushy, almost flat.

Mouse said, "You gotta hear me, Ruby, Joppy killed Frank."

"I ain't kilt Frankie!" Joppy cried.

"Why you keep callin' her that?" I asked.

"Me an' Frank known each other way back, Ease, 'fore I even met you. I remember old Ruby here from her baby days. Half-sister. She more filled out now but I never forget a face." Mouse pulled out a cigarette. "You know you a lucky man, Easy. I got it in mind to follah this mothahfuckah when I seen'im comin' outta yo' house this afternoon. I'as lookin' fo' you when I seen'im. I had Dupree's car so I follahed him downtown and he hooked up with whitey. Once I seed that you know I was on his ass for the duration."

I looked at Joppy. His eyes were big and he was sweating. Watery blood was dripping from his chin. "I ain't killed Frank, man. I ain't had no cause. Why I wanna kill Frank? Lissen, Ease, only reason I got you in this was so you could get some money—fo' that house."

"Then why you wit' Albright now?"

"She lied, man. Albright come t'me and he told me 'bout that money she got. She lied! She said she ain't hardly had no money!"

"Alright, thas enough talk," Mouse said. "Now, Ruby, I don't wanna scare ya but I will have that money."

"You don't scare me, Ray," she said simply.

Mouse frowned for just a second. It was like a small cloud

passing quickly on a sunny day. Then he smiled.

"Ruby, you gotta worry 'bout yourself now, honey. You know men can get desperate when it comes to money . . ." Mouse let his words trail off while he took the pistol from his waistband.

He turned casually to his right and shot Joppy in the groin. Joppy's eyes opened wide and he started honking like a seal. He rocked back and forth trying to grab his wound but the wires held him to the chair. After a few seconds Mouse leveled his pistol and shot Joppy in the head. One moment Joppy had two bulging eyes, then his left eye was just a bloody, ragged hole. The force of the second shot threw him to the floor; spasms went threw his legs and feet for minutes afterward. I felt cold then. Joppy had been my friend but I'd seen many men die and I cared for Coretta too.

Mouse stood up and said, "So let's go get that money, honey." He picked up her clothes from behind the couch and dropped the heap in her lap. Then he went out the front door.


"Help me, Easy." Her eyes were full of fear and promise. "He's crazy. You still have your gun."

"I can't," I said.

"Then give it to me. I'll do it."

That was probably the closest Mouse had ever come to a violent death.

"No."


"I found some blood in the road," Mouse said when he returned. "I tole ya I got'im. I don't know how bad it is but he gonna remember me." There was childish glee in his voice.

While he talked I untied Joppy's corpse. I took Mouse's jammed pistol and put it in Joppy's hand.

"What you doin', Easy?" Mouse asked.

"I don't know, Ray. Just confusing things I guess."

Daphne rode with me and Mouse followed in Dupree's car. When
we were a few miles away I threw Joppy's extension cord bonds
down an embankment.

"Did you kill Teran?" I asked as we swung onto Sunset Boulevard.

"I guess so," she said, so softly that I had to strain to hear her.

"You guess? You don't know?"

"I pulled the trigger, he died. But he killed himself really. I
went to him, to ask him to leave me alone. I offered him all my
money but he just laughed. He had his hands in that little boy's
drawers and he laughed." Daphne snorted. I don't know if it was
a laugh or a sound of disgust. "And so I killed him."

"What happened to the boy?"

"I brought him to my place. He just ran in the corner and
wouldn't even move."


Daphne had the bag in a YWCA locker.

Back in East L.A. Mouse counted out ten thousand for each of
us. He let Daphne keep the bag.

She called a cab and I went out with her to wait by the granite
lamppost at the curb.

"Stay with me," I said. Moths fluttered around us in that small
circle of light.

"I can't, Easy, I can't stay with you."

"Why not?" I asked.

"I just can't."

I put my hand out but she moved away saying, "Don't touch
me."

"I've done more than touch you, honey."

"That wasn't me."

"What you mean? Who was it if it wasn't you?" I moved toward
her and she got behind her bag.

"I'll talk to you, Easy. I'll talk to you till the car comes but just don't touch me. Don't touch me or I'll yell."

"What's wrong?"

"You know what's wrong. You know who I am; what I am."

"You ain't no different than me. We both just people, Daphne. That's all we are."

"I'm not Daphne. My given name is Ruby Hanks and I was born in Lake Charles, Louisiana. I'm different than you because I'm two people. I'm her *and* I'm me. I never went to that zoo, she did. She was there and that's where she lost her father. I had a different father. He came home and fell in my bed about as many times as he fell in my mother's. He did that until one night Frank killed him."

When she looked up at me I had the feeling that she wanted to reach out to me, not out of love or passion but to implore me.

"Bury Frank," she said.

"Okay. But you could stay here with me and we could bury him together."

"I can't. Do me one other favor?"

"What's that?"

"Do something about the boy."

I didn't really want her to stay. Daphne Monet was death herself. I was glad that she was leaving.

But I would have taken her in a second if she'd asked me to.

The cab driver could tell something was wrong. He kept looking around as if he expected to be mugged any second. She asked him to carry her bag. She put her hand on his arm to thank him but she wouldn't even shake my hand goodbye.


"Why'd you kill him, Mouse?"

"Who?"

"Joppy!"

Mouse was whistling and wrapping his money in a package fashioned from brown paper bags.

"He the cause of all yo' pain, Easy. And anyway, I needed to show that girl how serious I was."

"But she already hated him fo' Frank; maybe you could'a worked on that."

"It was me killed Frank," he said. This time it was Mouse reminding me of DeWitt Albright.

"You killed him?"

"So what? What you think he gonna do fo' you? You think he wasn't gonna kill you?"

"That don't mean I had t'kill'im."

"Hell it don't!" Mouse flashed his eyes angrily at me.

It was murder and I had to swallow it.

"You just like Ruby," Mouse said.

"What you say?"

"She wanna be white. All them years people be tellin' her how she light-skinned and beautiful but all the time she knows that she can't have what white people have. So she pretend and then she lose it all. She can love a white man but all he can love is the white girl he think she is."

"What's that got to do with me?"

"That's just like you, Easy. You learn stuff and you be thinkin' like white men be thinkin'. You be thinkin' that what's right fo' them is right fo' you. She look like she white and you think like you white. But brother you don't know that you both poor niggers. And a nigger ain't never gonna be happy 'less he accept what he is."

They found DeWitt Albright slumped over his steering wheel just north of Santa Barbara; it took him that long to bleed to death. I could hardly believe it. A man like DeWitt Albright didn't die, couldn't die. It frightened me even to think of a world that could kill a man like that; what could a world like that do to me?

Mouse and I heard it on the radio when I was driving him to the bus station the next morning. I was happy to see him off.

"I'm'a give all that money to Etta, Easy. Maybe she take me back now that I done saved yo' ass and come up rich." Mouse smiled at me and climbed on the bus. I knew I'd see him again and I didn't know how I felt about that.

That same morning I went to Daphne's apartment where I found the little boy. He was filthy. His underwear hadn't been changed in weeks and mucus was caked in his nose and on his face. He didn't say anything. I found him eating from a bag of flour in the kitchen. When I walked up to him and held out my hand he just took it and followed me to the bathroom. After he was clean I brought him out to Primo's place.

"I don't think he understands English," I said to Primo. "Maybe you could get something out of him."

Primo was a father at heart. He had as many children as Ronald White and he loved them all.

"I could give some mommasita a few hundred bucks over the next year or two while she looked after him," I said.

"I'll see," Primo said. He already had the boy in his lap. "Maybe I know someone."

The next person I went to see was Mr. Carter. He gave me a cool eye when I told him that Daphne was gone. I told him that I'd heard from Albright about the killings Joppy and Frank had done. I told him about Frank's death and that Joppy had disappeared.

But what really got to him was when I told him that I knew Daphne was colored. I told him that she wanted me to tell him that she loved him and wanted to be with him but that she would never know any kind of peace as long as she was with him. I laid it on kind of thick but he liked it that way.

I told him about her sundress, and while I talked I thought about making love to her when she was still a white woman. He had a look of ecstasy on his face; I had a darker feeling, but just as strong, inside.

"But I've got a problem, Mr. Carter, and you do too."

"Oh?" He was still savoring the last glimpse of her. "What is that?"

"I'm the only suspect that the police have," I told him. "And unless sumpin' happens I'm'a have to tell'em 'bout Daphne. And you know she gonna hate you if you drag her through the papers. She might even kill herself," I said. I didn't think it was a lie.

"What can I do about that?"

"You the one braggin' 'bout all your City Hall connections."

"Yes?"

"Then get'em on the phone. I got a story t'tell'em but you gotta back me up in it. 'Cause if I go in there on my own you know they gonna sweat me till I tell about Daphne."

"Why should I help you, Mr. Rawlins? I lost my money and my fiancée. You haven't done a thing for me."

"I saved her life, man. I let her get away with your money and her skin. Any one of the men involved with this would have seen her dead."

That very afternoon we went to City Hall and met with the assistant to the chief of police and the deputy mayor, Lawrence Wrightsmith. The policeman was short and fat. He looked to the deputy mayor before saying anything, even hello. The deputy mayor was a distinguished man in a gray suit. He waved his arm through the air while he talked and he smoked Pall Malls. He had silver-gray hair and I thought for a moment that he looked the way I imagined the president to be when I was a child.

Officers Mason and Miller were called when I mentioned them.

We were all sitting in Mr. Wrightsmith's office. He was behind his desk and the deputy police chief stood behind him. Carter and I sat before the desk and Carter's lawyer was behind us. Mason and Miller sat off to the side, on a couch.

"Well, Mr. Rawlins," Mr. Wrightsmith said. "You have something to tell us about all these murders going on?"

"Yessir."

"Mr. Carter here says that you were working for him."

"In a way, sir."

"What way is that?"

"I was hired by DeWitt Albright, through a friend of ours, Joppy Shag. Mr. Albright hired Joppy to locate Frank and Howard Green. And later on Joppy got him to hire me."

"Frank and Howard, eh? Brothers?"

"I've been told that they were distant cousins, but I couldn't swear to that," I said. "Mr. Albright wanted me to find Frank for Mr. Carter here. But he didn't tell me why he wanted them, just that it was business."

"It was for the money I told you about, Larry," Carter said. "You know."

Mr. Wrightsmith smiled and said to me, "Did you find them?"

"Joppy had already got to Howard Green, that's when he found out about the money."

"And what exactly was it that he found out, Mr. Rawlins?"

"Howard worked for a rich man, Matthew Teran. And Mr. Teran was mad because Mr. Carter here messed him up on running for mayor," I smiled. "I guess he was looking to be your boss."

Mr. Wrightsmith smiled too.

"Anyway," I continued, "he wanted Howard and Frank to kill Mr. Carter and make it look like a robbery. But when they got in the house and found that thirty thousand dollars they got so excited that they just ran without even doin' the job."

"What thirty thousand dollars?" Mason asked.

"Later," Wrightsmith said. "Did Joppy kill Howard Green?"

"That's what I think now. You see, I didn't get in it until they were looking for Frank. You see, DeWitt was checking out Mr. Teran because Mr. Carter suspected him. Then DeWitt got interested in the Greens when he checked out Howard and came up with Frank's name. He wanted somebody to look for Frank in the illegal bars down around Watts."

"Why were they looking for Frank?"

"DeWitt wanted him because he was lookin' for Mr. Carter's money, and Joppy wanted him for that thirty thousand dollars, for himself."

The sun was coming in on Mr. Wrightsmith's green blotter. I was sweating as if it was coming in on me.

"How did you find all this out, Easy?" Miller asked.

"From Albright. He got suspicious when Howard turned up dead and then he was certain when Coretta James was killed."

"Why's that?" Wrightsmith said. Every man in the room was staring at me. I had never been on trial but I felt I was up against the jury right then.

"Because they were looking for Coretta too. You see, she spent a lot of time around the Greens."

"Why didn't you get suspicious, Easy?" Miller asked. "Why didn't you tell us about this when we brought you in?"

"I didn't know none'a this when you talked to me. Albright and Joppy had me looking for Frank Green. Howard Green was already dead and what did I know about Coretta?"

"Go on, Mr. Rawlins," Mr. Wrightsmith said.

"I couldn't find Frank. No one knew where he was. But I heard a story about him though. People were sayin' that he was mad over the death of his cousin and that he was out for revenge. I think he went out after Teran. He didn't know nuthin' 'bout Joppy."

"So you think that Frank Green killed Matthew Teran?" Miller couldn't hide his disgust. "And Joppy got to Frank Green and DeWitt Albright?"

"All I know is what I just said," I said as innocently as I could.

"What about Richard McGee? He stab himself?" Miller was out of his chair.

"I don't know 'bout him," I said.

They asked me questions for a couple of hours more. The story stayed the same though. Joppy did most of the killing. He did it out of greed. I went to Mr. Carter when I heard about DeWitt's death and he decided to come to the police.

When I finished Wrightsmith said, "Thank you very much, Mr. Rawlins. Now if you'll just excuse us."

Mason and Miller, Jerome Duffy—Carter's lawyer, and I all had to go.

Duffy shook my hand and smiled at me. "See you at the inquest, Mr. Rawlins."

"What's that mean?"

"Just a formality, sir. When a serious crime is committed they want to ask a few questions before closing the books."

It didn't sound any worse than a parking ticket if you listened to him.

He got in the elevator to leave and Mason and Miller went with him.

I took the stairs. I thought I might even walk all the way home. I had two years' salary buried in the back yard and I was free. No one was after me; not a worry in my life. Some hard things had happened but life was hard back then and you just had to take the bad along with the worse if you wanted to survive.

Miller came up to me as I descended the granite stair of City Hall.

"Hi, Ezekiel."

"Officer."

"You got a mighty powerful friend up there."

"I don't know what you mean," I said, but I did know.

"You think Carter gonna come save your ass when we arrest you every other day for jaywalking, spitting, and creating a general nuisance? Think he's gonna answer your calls?"

"Why I have to worry about that?"

"You have to worry, Ezekiel"—Miller pushed his thin face right up to mine; he smelled of bourbon, wintermint, and sweat—"because I have to worry."

"What do you have to worry about?"

"I got a prosecutor, Ezekiel. He's got a fingerprint that don't belong to anybody we know."

"Maybe it's Joppy's. Maybe when you find him you'll have it."

"Maybe. But Joppy's a boxer. Why'd he stop boxing to use a knife?"

I didn't know what to say.

"Give it to me, son. Give it to me and I'll let you off. I'll forget about the *coincidence* of you being involved in all this and having drinks with Coretta the night before she died. Mess with me and I'll see that you spend the rest of your life in jail."

"You could try Junior Fornay against that print."

"Who?"

"Bouncer at John's. He might fit it."

It might be that the last moment of my adult life, spent free, was in that walk down the City Hall stairwell. I still remember the stained-glass windows and the soft light.

**31**

"I guess things turned out okay, huh, Easy?"

"What?" I turned away from watering my dahlias. Odell was nursing a can of ale.

"Dupree's okay and the police got the killers."

"Yeah."

"But, you know, something bothers me."

"What's that, Odell?"

"Well, it's been three months, Easy, an' you ain't had a job or looked for one far as I can see."

The San Bernadino range is the most beautiful in the fall. The high winds get rid of all the smog and the skies take your breath away.

"I been workin'."

"You got a night job?"

"Sometimes."

"What you mean, sometimes?"

"I work for myself now, Odell. And I got two jobs."

"Yeah?"

"I bought me a house, on auction for unpaid taxes, and I been rentin' it and—"

"Where you get that kinda money?"

"Severance from Champion. And you know them taxes wasn't all that much."

"What's your other job?"

"I do it when I need a few dollars. Private investigations."

"Git away from here!"

"No lie."

"Who you work for?"

"People I know and people they know."

"Like who?"

"Mary White is one of 'em."

"What you do for her?"

"Ronald run off on her two months back. I tailed him up to Seattle and gave her the address. Her family brought him back down."

"What else?"

"I found Ricardo's sister in Galveston and told her what Rosetta was doin' with 'im. She gave me a few bucks when she come up and set him free."

"Damn!" That was the only time I ever heard Odell curse. "That sounds like some dangerous business, man."

"I guess. But you know a man could end up dead just crossin' the street. Least this way I say I earned it."


Later on that evening Odell and I were having a dinner I threw together. We were sitting out front because it was still hot in L.A.

"Odell?"

"Yeah, Easy."

"If you know a man is wrong, I mean, if you know he did somethin' bad but you don't turn him in to the law because he's your friend, do you think that's right?"

"All you got is your friends, Easy."

"But then what if you know somebody else who did something wrong but not so bad as the first man, but you turn this other guy in?"

"I guess you figure that that other guy got ahold of some bad luck."

We laughed for a long time.